REAWAKENED WORLDS

VOLUME TWO

Introduced by Laurie Winslow Sargent

JOHN HAYDEN HOWARD

WILDBLUE
PRESS

WildBluePress.com

REAWAKENED WORLDS, VOLUME TWO
published by: WILDBLUE PRESS

P.O. Box 102440
Denver, Colorado 80250

Foreword and Afterword by Laurie Winslow Sargent, TTEE for John H. Howard

ISBN 978-1-960332-35-6 Trade Paperback
ISBN 978-1-960332-33-2 eBook
ISBN 978-1-960332-34-9 Hardback

Cover design © 2023 WildBlue Press. All rights reserved.

Interior Formatting and Cover Design by Elijah Toten
www.totencreative.com

REAWAKENED
WORLDS

This book is dedicated to all fans of Hayden Howard,
honoring his name and creativity for over half a century.

ACKNOWLEDGEMENTS

From Laurie: Thanks to all who offered insights or transcription assistance for this book, including my beloved NC Scribes critique group, Sylvia and Mark Sanderson, and my forever cheerleader Cyndi Moor Jones. I'm thankful for the enduring support of my husband of 44 years, as meeting book deadlines always means him scrounging in the refrigerator for something edible while tolerating creep of my own paper piles throughout our house. I also appreciate my family's hoarding tendencies, resulting in old papers being saved for over half a century—to find new life in *Reawakened Worlds*.

Contents

FOREWORD

By
Laurie Winslow Sargent

Welcome to Volume Two of *Reawakened Worlds*, which will take you on a new journey fifty to seventy years back in time. Pack your bags and prepare to time-travel.

As in Vol One of this series, here you'll find dystopian (sometimes utopian) and science fiction stories, written between 1950 and 1977 by internationally known author John Hayden Howard (1925-2014). Yet what makes this particular volume unique is that these stories wrap ecopolitical concerns of that past era into futuristic and other-worldly, what-if, tales told with wry humor.

During the 1950s and 1960s, now known as The Golden Age of Sci-Fi, pulp science fiction magazines were tremendously popular. Under the pen name Hayden Howard, Jack (as I, his stepdaughter, called him) wrote for *Galaxy Science Fiction, IF Worlds of Science Fiction, ANALOG Science Fiction and Fact, Planet Stories*, and other magazines, including *Tales of the Sea* and *Ellery Queen Mystery Magazine*.

Most of his 73 published short stories and novelettes (including foreign language translations) are listed at ISFDB.org, the Internet Speculative Fiction Database. Hayden Howard is also referenced in the *Encyclopedia of Science Fiction*. He was best known in the 1960s for his novel *The Eskimo Invasion*, a finalist for the 1967 Nebula Award, a story about a strange alien invasion of villagers in the Canadian Arctic. (His related novelette was in Vol. One: "Arctic Invasion.")

As you read these stories, you may need to pinch yourself occasionally as a reminder that Jack imagined all the futuristic tech in his stories over sixty years ago. Think back to the age of bulky typewriters. Picture him rolling out a sheet of paper from his typewriter to scribble in its margins, then inserting a fresh page to retype each corrected passage. Personal computers were only a dream.

Consider how he got his news—perhaps from Walter Cronkite's evening news program on black-and-white televisions housed in giant wooden consoles. Or from newspapers—the *Los Angeles Times*, the *Santa Barbara News-Press*, or *St. Augustine Record*. He loved to weave bits of news he'd heard into wild stories.

Most of his stories predated man's landing on the moon in 1969. Yet from Hayden Howard's wild imagination emerged characters flying between planets. Other characters videochatted on "visaphones," and drove electric cars in solar-powered cities. One character even appears to vape from an "Everbreathe" cigar, while another character flies in a "jetcopter" described much like the Osprey military helicopter invented twenty years later.

It took effort on my part to properly date stories in this collection, particularly those not previously published. To do so, I compared the author's various addresses (typed on his original manuscripts) to census records. Those records showed where he lived and when, at least during the times when the U.S. Census was taken (every ten years). I also used correspondence from Howard's literary agent, Scott Meredith, to date stories that don't appear in magazine databases. It's possible, however, some seemingly unpublished works were in other vintage magazines not yet archived online.

There is currently fresh fascination with 1950s and 1960s science fiction works, with many stories from that era now made into modern feature films and television programs. Philip K. Dick's *Man in the High Castle*, written back in 1962, is now a fascinating streaming television series. The movie *The Adjustment Bureau*, with Matt Damon, was based off of Dick's original story "Adjustment Team"—first published in 1954, in *Orbit Science Fiction* magazine. Isaac Asimov's *Foundation* series, written in the 1940s-1950s, was recently adapted to film.

Around the same time Hayden Howard was nominated for prestigious science fiction awards (Nebula and Hugo Awards), so were authors Philip K. Dick, Isaac Asimov, and J. R.R. Tolkien, as were original Star Trek episodes. It certainly was a golden era.

It's strange reading some of Howard's stories in this volume which have strong themes of energy conservation, the space race, and spies—concerns which still resonate with us a half-century later. Some phrases he used in his stories catch me by surprise as they are often used in 2024. Yet I promise that I never put those words in his mouth—nor his writing. Most of my editing for this volume consisted of correcting my own typos—or what I call, "speakos," when dictating stories from his original manuscripts.

Sometimes even after multiple copyedits, the author's extremely subtle humor has caught me off guard. I slapped my forehead this very week, suddenly making a connection with one phrase. In Howard's 500 Points story, the creator of the futuristic computer's name was Niel S. Gallroper. (Yes: Nielsen Ratings and the Gallup Poll did exist in 1950.) I love how sometimes days after I read a story of his I suddenly get it. His story title "Oil-Mad Bug-Eyed Monsters," I had shortened to "Oil-Mad," then suddenly I realized its significance. It is humans who are the monsters. Pay attention to the initials on the alien salesman's briefcase.

The following roadmap may help you anticipate, as you travel through the nine stories, how long each leg of your journey will take. I also noted for you the strange places you'll go, and characters you'll meet along the way:

In PART 1: DECEPTIVE DIGNITARIES, the first story is the novelette, "Kendy," written in 1968. It was originally titled "Kendy's World" when published in *Galaxy Science Fiction* magazine in 1969. It was later reprinted in French, in 1974, as "Le monde de Kendy."

Kendy, a California high school student, is recruited by a strange man to attend a modern, futuristic-tech, government university. Meanwhile, the Russians are doing mysterious things on the moon. Kendy is flown by jetcopter up the California coast to a secret location near San Louis Obispo, then persuaded through promises and flattery to enroll. But eventually our naïve young man learns that his recruitment was not what it seemed.

Next up is "500 Points for Father Image," a brief tale written sometime in the late 1950s.

In this fun short-short story, the presidential incumbent and his competing candidate take turns speaking to the public via television. While viewers watch, a Big Screen attached to a computer scores the candidates' speeches word by word, simultaneously tallying scores. The Big Screen then chooses who becomes President of the United States. (In this AI world we live in now, this may not seem such an odd idea anymore.)

"Counterattack" is another brief story packed with references that will make you pinch yourself, as previously suggested. The story was written in 1951, back when Jack was only 26 years old. (Had he lived past age 89, he'd now be 98 years old.) Yet his character uses technology that we only regularly use now.

Next up comes PART TWO: TOUCHY TECHNOLOGY. In the novelette "I've Got to Save JFK," a character is desperate to change history. The general premise of this story—preventing the assassination of John F. Kennedy—may remind you of Stephen King's 2011 novel (and the television series) 11/22/63. However, John Hayden Howard wrote his story in 1977, thirty-four years before King's novel was published. Also, in King's 2011 story, a man travels back to the 60's repeatedly to try to change the future. In Hayden Howard's 1977 story, an inventor sets up a device in modern-day Dallas (in this story, "modern" being 1993) pointing to where Oswald presumably fired his fatal shot. The scientist's goal is to send a laser beam into the past to alter the path of the bullet. Assuming Kennedy survives, that would create a new 1993 future.

Twice his plan fails, with major repercussions. As for his third attempt? Well, you shall see! As you think back to your own life in 1993, it's interesting seeing three alternates of that year.

Next, in the 1960s short story "The March of Time" college students are engaged in a science experiment. One takes it too far. Over the three decades, the former students take paths, including political, which eventually converge in one bizarre, unexpected moment. 1960s slang and political references abound in this story, with one minor character briefly demanding that pot be legalized. As if *that* would ever happen, right?

"Breakout," the following quick story, offers us a humorous break. The character is a greedy man attempting a major heist at Fort Knox, using an unusual invention. His comeuppance in the end is oddly satisfying.

In PART 3: COSMIC ECOPOLITICS, you will meet in the short story, "Oil-Mad, Bug-Eyed Monsters" an alien posing as an attractive salesman to persuade a homeowner to sell her home on oil-rich land. Prior to writing this, Hayden

Howard was no doubt impacted by the infamous 1969 Santa Barbara oil spill, which had occurred off the coast of his own beloved city.

Previously published in *Galaxy Science Fiction*, that story was later reprinted in the anthology *Best SF: 1970*. Note, as you read the story, how the salesman attempts to use guilt, greed, blame, fear, statistics, and fawning to get the contract signed. (Sound like any salesmen who've knocked on your door? Beware—they may not be human!) To fit in *Reawakened Worlds*, in this condensed version a few tangential scenes were removed to focus on Hayden Howard's main story.

Next comes a longer story, "To Grab Power," originally in *IF Science Fiction and Fact* magazine in 1971, later in an anthology edited by Isaac Asimov. To best fit in *Reawakened Worlds*, this story was condensed while all other original wording was retained. The plot follows the alarming realization that someone—possibly a beloved friend—was ejected prematurely from a space shuttle. There is a race to see if that man survived, or to uncover what evil plot had him cast out. But this story is also about political extremes and how those came about on one instaplanet, created from once-utopian dreams.

The final story in this volume is the short story "The Last Surfer," written in the early 1970s. It's set in a strange futuristic government-controlled society, which claims to boost Earth's natural resources. An employee discovers that oil is being siphoned from Earth and sent elsewhere. Where? On his surfboard, he follows a conduit to a strange place, then realizing that to save Earth he must make a wild and final ride.

When I began sorting through John Hayden Howard's old manuscripts, as his executor, I internet-searched his published works. It startled me at first to realize that he still has fans a half-century later. Five of his 1950s stories, in the past few years, fell into public domain. Those stories were transcribed, then uploaded, by Project Gutenberg, which I appreciated—as transcription takes work. Of those public domain stories, I find "The Ethic of the Assassin" most intriguing. I hope you enjoy reading that at Project Gutenberg.

Meanwhile, those same stories ("Murder Beneath the Polar Ice," "The Luminous Blonde," "The Un-Reconstructed Woman," "It," and "The Ethic of the Assassin") have now been copied—repeatedly—by unknown publishers. I only think it worth mentioning because I'd like you to have confidence that *Reawakened Worlds* is the only official collection from the original manuscripts and estate of John Hayden Howard. More importantly, this book also includes never-before-seen 1950s stories which are not in public domain plus other stories not seen for fifty to sixty years.

I'm thankful the author trusted me with his estate, including his literary works, as his executor. I still recall the day in 1989, when as a young adult I met "Jack" who then married my widowed mother. For decades, as his stepdaughter, I loved that gregarious, kind man.

When I inherited his musty dusty yellowed manuscripts and began compiling them for MacGregor Literary to sell to WildBlue Press, I originally called the compilation *Hidden Stories*. After all, the stories had seemingly been forgotten in the back of a closet for sixty to seventy years. However, I love the revised title *Reawakened Worlds* as these stories reawaken memories and stories from many decades ago. I sincerely hope you enjoy this new set of old tales and your trip back in time.

PART 1: DECEPTIVE DIGNITARIES

KENDY

A novelette, written in 1968
Previously in *Galaxy Science Fiction* magazine, 1969
Setting: A strange California university

A t first Kendy guessed the Russians were as paranoid
as Americans. Their armor of systemized delusions
about the nature of the universe had been penetrated by
something. They were uptight.

Their *Lotka II* had attached herself to Phobos moon,
with passengers including the prominent biochemist E.
Vavlov. However, the Russian landing module never did
spiral down to the nearby fascinating surface of Mars. All
three silvery modules of *Lotka* instead clung to that lifeless
moonlet. Whenever Phobos whirled from behind Mars,
coded lasergrams flickered.

After official secrecy dense enough to shield ideological
confusion, Moscow announced a minor technical difficulty.
Lotka had returned all three men to Earth, yet there was no
interview with E. Vavilov.

Kendy, at age sixteen, was momentarily interested,
but felt all that had nothing to do with him. His personal
universe was small. He wanted to be a basketball coach.
Or a biochemist. Perhaps a statesman? While his friends
casually smoked grass, he felt fragmented.

I n the hospital delivery room, his gasping young mother had hoped he'd become the groovy swinger his father wasn't. His father, a caseworker for the Welfare Department, hoped instead that little smiling ape-face would become President of the United States.

But his father didn't live long. His skull had been shattered by a stray bullet the day the National Emergency was declared. Kendy was seven then. Now all he could remember about that day was smoke spreading from downtown Los Angeles. He didn't remember crying, nor remember his father's voice. He couldn't remember the feel of his father's hand on his shoulder.

Clutching the family photo album, he often stared at his father's two-dimensional face in glossy photographs. Under a magnifying glass, that face disintegrated into blotches and specs, as if his father hid from him.

Or perhaps he hid from his father, not wanting to wrestle with who or what killed him. His father's unobtrusive last name had been Olson. The Los Angeles telephone directories contained thousands of living fathers named Olson. Why was he the one to die?

His mother tried to explain. "He was very sentimental and idealistic."

Then she rambled. "I guess I was what they called…a hippie. When we brought you home from the hospital, I started calling you Ken for short. Your father laughed. He said, 'Reminds me too much of those Ken and Barbie dolls. We named him Kendy—we'll call him Kendy. He'll be proud of it!'"

When she said that, although Kendy couldn't remember his father, he remembered that in Kindergarten other children had trouble pronouncing his name. One day he was exuberantly leading the children up and down on chairs, until his teacher argued that it was rest time. But instead of sprawling on his rest mat with eyes shut, he had tried to read the rustling pages of the Los Angeles Times. He was matching the letters M O L with a photo of that Manned Orbiting Laboratory when the teacher's weak voice had shifted from reprimand to sing-song ridicule. To his surprise, all the other children had chanted with her: "Kendy reads a noisy newspaper, Kendy reads a noisy newspaper."

Kendy had folded that terribly loud newspaper and feared that no one would like him anymore. He soon learned to get a Gold Star for cooperation in school.

By the time Kendy turned sixteen, the National Emergency had been in effect for nine years. His society was full of mistrust of intellectualism in a world of paranoids, yet he barely noticed it. He'd grown up with it.

A gangling six-footer with floppy brownish hair, he stood in contrast to his plump mother with raven-black hair. She was one-quarter Mescalero Apache and had high Asian cheekbones, which Kendy inherited. But Kendy's fair skin came from his Minnesota-Swedish father. An ethnologist might shrug and jokingly classify him as *Sibersk*, a Soviet citizen from the Siberian racial melting pot.

His high cheekbones made him appear to squint, yet he smiled so much in contrast to the cool expressions of his classmates, they were attracted to him. Last year he had been elected Sophomore Class President. This year he was a hard-working member of the student council, and hustled on the Junior Varsity basketball team, bounding down court like a grasshopper. He smiled at his teachers, wanting to like them—but when not around them spoke like an uneducated slob.

He couldn't help laughing whenever he realized his life was a put-on. By letting his grades slump, he had become more popular with the kids than the teachers. He ran for student body president, surprising everyone by presenting a political platform as if it were a real election, concerned with real power. His number one plank was yearly grading of teachers by their students. Hopefully, constructive criticism would be conducted and tabulated off campus. He worried a little that he might actually be elected.

On the television news, he saw that Soviet space efforts had been redirected to Earth's garbage-strewn moon. In a startling retreat from their Phobos-Mars copout, they were conducting a massive re-exploration of Earth's moon. Soviet crawlers searched its maria and craters so intensively they seemed insane. They had even upgraded the abandoned U.S. base. Nothing on the moon could be worth as much as that search was costing.

Meanwhile, in West Virginia, the Tin Woodman telescope—overshadowing Ozma II in its search for extraterrestrial intelligence via interstellar radio waves—was dynamited by persons unknown. Tin Woodman was considered a menace by paranoids of various political persuasions who were afraid something out there might hear Tin Woodman's refined radio shouts to the universe.

K endy felt both relieved and angered when notified he'd lost the school election—by three stinking votes. Loping down the long concrete steps from the campus, he wished he could escape from high school. Ahead of him for next November, his Senior year now crystal-balled as a drag. He doubted he could make the Senior Varsity basketball team. He might run for Biochem Club president but needed to resuscitate his grades before college recruiters returned.

Kendy wandered outside of the high school's chain-link fence to where a tall jovial man stood.

"How'd the election come out?" Mr. Smith resembled a college basketball coach on a recruiting expedition.

"Down the tubes," Kendy retorted.

Mr. Smith had taken him to lunch all week until today.

"I'll wear a black arm band." Mr. Smith laughed unexpectedly. He glanced down at his brown shoes, which were peculiarly small and short for such a huge man. "Seriously, I heard you lost by only three votes."

"Then why'd you ask me how it came out?" Kendy blurted. "The count hasn't even been announced yet, except to me and Steve."

"I was anxious." Mr. Smith grinned, tightening his jowls until he appeared to be well-conditioned forty-five.

"For me to lose?" Kendy knew why that was true.

"Ken—Kendy, I've been trying too hard to impress you." His smile became so uncertain he could've passed for a dissipated thirty-five, then so enthusiastic it seemed a slimmer man of twenty-five peeked out. "Since you've lost, since you're cutting afternoon classes anyway, fly up with me past San Luis Obispo right now, for a grand tour. Why wait till next year?"

Kendy laughed, trying not to seem embarrassed. "You guys—recruiting kids before they even finish eleventh grade."

It didn't seem ethical. Kendy had only taken the Scholastic Aptitude Test as practice for next year's test. To his surprise, nineteen universities had contacted him prematurely. Academic recruiters slipped him glossy promotional booklets, advising him to 'stay clean' until as a Senior he could sign their Letter of Intent.

Good students were more actively recruited than athletes, since Senate Bill 30-06 had passed—the year the National Emergency began. It doubled tuition subsidies to any approved university for each student recruited whose scores were at least 500 in English and 650 in Math. Senators had added other requirements. Approved recruits must be patriotic high school graduates.

"I won't have enough units to get my high school diploma until next June," Kendy said.

"That makes us a better choice than Harvard," Mr. Smith laughed. "We want you now."

Kendy had heard that this new National University wasn't dependent on emergency education legislation. With unlimited government funding, it set its own entrance criteria.

"I've lost the election," Kendy said. "Why do you still want me?"

He didn't know if *he* wanted National U. The UCLA recruiter had knocked NU even worse than USC. His high school counselor warned him that enrolling at National University was like making a deal with the devil, then weakened his argument by pushing his own alma mater, Fresno State. The National Television Station commentators all said National University had outstanding educational innovations.

Mr. Smith rested his gray-gloved hand on Kendy's shoulder. "Some fancy universities try to collect nothing but high school student-body presidents. But I kid you not, we just want guys we like."

Cornball, Kendy thought, but smiled, liking Mr. Smith better and better.

The gray glove pressing on Kendy's shoulders seemed smooth, but its weight transmitted a strange bumpy feeling. Yesterday, when Mr. Smith had taken him to lunch, Kendy felt uncomfortable watching him munch a cheeseburger while wearing gloves. But he wore a groovy next-year's sports coat with a long Edwardian tail, so must be a smooth operator despite forgetting to remove his gloves when he ate.

"Say the word, Kendy. We'll take a taxi to the jet pad."

"Sir, I've got to be honest with you." Kendy blurted. "You'd better recruit some Senior. My mother will never sign the waiver to let me skip my last year of high school. She hates—"

"She'll fly up with us."

"You're kidding." Kendy knew his mother would refuse to visit that campus. Just last night she'd put another underground magazine on his pillow with an article roasting National University.

"Today at noon I took her to lunch at the Hilton," Mr. Smith explained.

"Are you putting me on?"

"Say the word, and I'll hustle back to the May Company. I can fix it with her supervisor so she can take the rest of the afternoon off, then we'll go." Mr. Smith spoke excitedly, as if twenty-five again. "What department is she in?"

"Complaints Department."

Kendy thought Mr. Smith overconfident. He couldn't understand him. He understood the surface of his words since Mr. Smith talked bluntly yet casually. But sometimes he'd switch—mouthing long, well-organized sentences, probably a recruiting spiel he'd rehearsed. That didn't necessarily indicate intelligence.

At times while kidding around, Mr. Smith wised-off so shrewdly that Kendy thought this huge man might be able to speak from a great depth of experience. Still, he sensed Mr. Smith's uncertainty—as if recruiting in a world he didn't quite believe in. Kendy wasn't repelled by this, since he too felt torn.

At home, his mother often spoke as if uneducated, but then would astonish him with her bitter wit. She seemed to be the only person who remembered what life was like before the National Emergency. At school, his friends were lazy slobs—unambitious and directionless—only half-hearted rebels. Meanwhile, Kendy's counselor, while berating him for not trying harder scholastically, would suddenly switch to praise. In those moments when the counselor shoveled child psychology on him like manure, Kendy also felt glowing moments of hope—hope that he might be capable, strong, and purposeful. Had his father been that way?

II

A t 2:32 the copter howled upward through the smog. Mr. Smith sat by Kendy's mother, shouting: "National University's a whole new concept in American education."

Her wide face flushed with excitement. In the roaring draft from the ventilator, her dark hair lashed her cheek. Kendy wondered how much Mr. Smith had researched his family history. Did he know that Kendy's mother, after only one semester at UCLA, had married a skinny, blonde-bearded sociology student, then left school to give birth to Kendy? If so, Dr. Smith might underestimate his mother.

"Only three of us in this big helicopter?" she shouted. She didn't seem to believe the cordless intercom on her tight headset worked. "Only three?"

"Holds fourteen," Mr. Smith answered proudly in a steady voice. "This is the newest Cheyennette," he continued innocently. "Fourteen seats in our passenger capsule. Comfortable?"

Kendy winced. He knew what was coming. His mother had a caustic tongue.

"I thought this so-called Coalition Congress," she shouted, "was hanging on for nine years—or ninety-nine—to save money! 'A dollar saved means a policeman's paid.' 'Let the poor pay for war.' I thought one reason for continuing the National Emergency was economy in government transportation."

To this sarcastic shaft, Mr. Smith merely explained, "The copter has to return to National University anyway."

Kendy looked away. If his mother kept making subversive remarks against the Coalition Congress, he might not be admitted to any university.

"Diplomats of the future," Mr. Smith said hopefully, "are getting their starts at National University."

"Kendy had a nice offer from Harvard," she shouted, "for next year—when he's ready."

Embarrassed, Kendy peered out his greasy window. He watched the stub-winged shadow of their copter slide across Santa Monica Bay and shrink as the Cheyennette rose. With its rotor blades clattering, the winged copter leveled off, then accelerated like an airplane. Kendy supposed its rotor was freewheeling now. Its deep tail propeller pushed them so fast the stubby wings surfboarded on the air.

Below, along the curve of Malibu beach, the surf wrinkled and whitened. Mr. Smith winked at him. Kendy hoped they were still friends. The winged copter buffeted northward, above the Santa Barbara Channel. Oil drilling platforms below looked like spiders standing in the greenish summer water.

The Cheyennette whined like a mosquito with its course paralleling the summer-brown Channel Islands. On San Miguel Island, Kendy noticed rows of black spots, probably barracks in the old Emergency Detention Camp. When his mother didn't seem to notice them, he relaxed. She was quieter than expected.

The Cheyennette began swaying like a boat. Ahead, the greenish water of the channel was streaked by an arctic blue current. Wind from the north stretched out the whitecaps. They passed over Point Conception, then Point Arguello. Between there and Vandenberg Air Force Base, Kendy saw brown hills with rows of excavations into underlying chalk like more whitecaps. He noticed radar dishes and unrecognizable apparatus, then realized that satellites must hover over many places besides Moscow and Washington D.C.

"We're almost there," Mr. Smith announced, perhaps to keep them from becoming restless.

Below, Kendy saw a long freight train flowing across a bridge. It wormed past pencil-sized Minute Man VII missiles standing at attention for testing. The shadow of one was enormous.

Kendy was jarred back to what must have been an ongoing conversation as Mr. Smith said, "...their intelligence operations weren't any better than ours, but before the emergency, our space appropriations were too small."

"When I was a girl, we always blamed spies," Kendy's mother replied dryly.

"That was about atoms, not rockets," Kendy blurted in embarrassment. As the train crawled past a concrete block house, he recalled viewing in class an American History tape about the old days when trains still carried passengers. On this same track, the Southern Pacific Daylight had rushed a Premier Krush-off-or-shev-or-something toward San Francisco, porters scurrying to pull blinds when the train passed by the air force base.

"For some reason they're crawling all over the moon again," Mr. Smith said.

"Why worry about the Russians, when it's us we should worry about?" his mother protested.

Kendy remembered his mother intently watching the Telstar broadcast the day the Russians sent those three men almost to Mars. They had seemed so confident. That grinning biochemist E. Vavilov announced what he expected to find on Mars. On the television screen, he seemed surprisingly young for a Nobel Prize winner. His high cheekbones made him appear somewhat Siberian.

"He looks like someone I know," Kendy's mother had muttered.

E. Vavilov had smiled mischievously while explaining his theory of a scientific doorway to understanding life throughout the universe. Did Vavilov mean to wink at all his friendly-enemy biochemists, out in worldwide television land? Then he *had* winked—or something got in his eye.

After his abortive return from space, E. Vavilov didn't appear on television again. Instead, the *Lotka II* pilot read excuses from his teleprompter: a minor technical difficulty. A month later, while maintaining either skills or flight pay, that pilot reportedly crashed his jet trainer. *Pravda* announced that E. Vavilov had returned to do research at the Limnological Institute on Lake Baikal, so was temporarily indisposed. Mars was not mentioned.

Meanwhile, the Soviets' inexplicable search of the rough surface of Earth's Moon had seemed an advance to the rear.

T he Cheyennette skimmed above the sand dunes of Pismo Beach, then banked oceanward around the dark cliffs of Port Avila. They must be approaching National University. Kendy smiled nervously. Mr. Smith had mentioned that NU was in a canyon, but Kendy only saw mountainous areas gashed by steep canyons down to the breakers.

"That's Diablo Canyon, Pacific Gas and Electric's nuke-electric generating plant," Mr. Smith said. "National U's so close that our lightbulbs stay lit by induction." He smiled faintly at the tired joke.

Mr. Smith pointed. "Northeast of here, our boys have fun assaulting—I mean, climbing—Moro Rock. Of course, the Park Service installed safety fences all the way to the top, so it's safe enough.

"Inland from here you can see San Luis Obispo—a nice little town of fifty thousand. See the Cal Poly campus? Those unimaginative engineers are supposed to be our sports rivals. They win football games but can't compete intellectually or beat our educational methods and architecture. NU stands alone—the model for the future of American higher education," Mr. Smith recited as if from the catalog. "…as an answer to the National Emergency. Congress has been generous—we're enlarging again this year."

Kendy saw below them a vast, shallow, bowl-shaped green pasture near what must have been a canyon before earth-moving machines did their work. Its bulldozed rim shimmered golden brown with wild oats. Small, red-tiled roofs surrounded a central hub of larger ones. Kendy blinked in surprise. Although it was 3:30 in the afternoon, the buildings cast oddly short shadows.

The circling Cheyennette jerked as its rotor reengaged. While descending, Kendy counted twenty tile-roofed buildings around the rim of the campus, with nine more dorms under construction. Yet even the huge buildings at the hub were only one story high, explaining their short shadows.

From the small buildings, which Kendy assumed were dorms, red tile paths traveled like spokes to the larger hub. Yet as the copter settled to land, Kendy saw no students on those paths. Inside glinting windows, administrative offices seemed to occupy the entire main building. Mystified, Kendy wondered: is everyone here an administrator?

A s they walked in past Spanish ironwork and dented armor, Kendy's mother asked, "Where will he sleep? Not even room for a hundred students."

The catalog had said each dorm could house 800.

Mr. Smith laughed. "We met requirements for historic California architecture and also met our country's needs." He led them to a row of elevator doors, all inscribed: DOWN.

At the minus-one level, they exited into what resembled a miniature railway station. An electric car hummed in from a central hub. Men scrambled off, none with beards or long hair. Surprisingly, few carried books.

Another car zipped through on a cross-track. Kendy straightened, as the car left a whiff of perfume.

"Well, that's something!" Kendy's mother said enigmatically. "When I was at UCLA, we had to hike miles between classes—always hurrying and always late. Is this a coeducational dorm?"

"Just passing through," Mr. Smith answered quickly. "Their car is on the rim track. They're just passing through to their own dorm. No girls are allowed below this level."

"That seems stupid," she remarked. "For a supposedly modern—"

"National University was authorized by Congress to rebuild moral standards," Mr. Smith hastily answered with a straight face. "Our goal is to renovate the traditional way of life which made America great." He grinned at Kendy. "But there are some cute girls here."

Kendy had known from the catalog there were only two women's dorms but hadn't given sufficient thought to the implications of that.

"...group solidarity within each dorm," Mr. Smith was still chatting, "and friendly supervision, like an enlightened academy. Student unrest, prevalent in older universities before the Emergency, can't happen here."

"Uh-huh," Kendy's mother said, in obvious disbelief.

"Over here," Mr. Smith said hastily, "is our recreation hall."

The clicking ping-pong ball on an automatic return table stopped. At the open end of one table, concealed nearly to the armpits, a startling young boy stared across the dark green plywood at Kendy. As if in disbelief or pain, the boy's sharp features screwed up.

Kendy squinted in recognition and opened his mouth to speak.

Oliver abruptly turned his back, and Kendy didn't know what to say. He heard Oliver gulp while walking away, big white tennis shoes flapping on the hardwood floor. Like Gollum, Kendy thought. When Oliver reached the dark doorway, he looked back, glaring.

Why? Kendy was sure *he* should be the one carrying the grudge.

Sweating, Kendy tried to feel angry. It wasn't rational to be afraid of a kid that small. He doubted Oliver was even fourteen yet. But he was evidently enrolled here, with the advantage of being in a higher grade. Kendy reassured himself that NU wasn't like West Point, with hazing of plebes and all that guff. Anyway, he was only visiting. He was not committed to enroll here.

But if he turned chicken, Kendy thought, and didn't sign up just because Oliver was here, he'd be both timid and stupid. Oliver was only a little—well, what was he?

III

M r. Smith deftly steered Kendy's mother down the hall away from a door to a dim room barred by steel grillwork, labeled Trophy Room. Kendy peered through the locked grill at dim shapes of rifles hanging on the walls. He recognized the awkward silhouette of an ancient Chicomm AK-47 with its forward-curving magazine. Other guns were new to him. His heart pounded. Rows of glass cases glinted, but he couldn't see what they contained. From one rifle in the wall hung wires and a battery. He itched to hold one, but hurried away, feeling a need to escape something.

The coffee-teria reeked with the odor of burning cheese. A tall man in a sharp sportscoat was scraping a smoking cheese sandwich from an infrared dispenser. He seemed to be another recruiter, as a mother, father, and son sat at one round table with four coffee cups but only two sandwiches. They looked around uncomfortably.

To his surprise, Kendy's mother smiled. Mr. Smith had brought her a lunch with everything she liked best. As Kendy moved to join them, Mr. Smith removed his arm from behind her chair. He pointed Kendy to the gleaming row of snack dispensers. "You don't need coins; help yourself."

Feeling like a third wheel, Kendy went to the infrared dispenser. He pushed buttons, hoping to force the machine to grill him a sandwich. It hummed.

A past image of Oliver loomed in his memory, as if the kid were a monster.

Two summers ago, Oliver would have been only twelve when Kendy was a counselor at that camp for gifted children. Kendy had been conducting a first inspection in his tribe's tent. He saw Oliver slouched behind his messy cot, gulping air to contemptuously belch. Although Kendy didn't bother to make his own bed at home, he tried to enforce camp rules. Fold the sheet over; blanket corners must be square. In response, Oliver blurted a four-letter word. Kendy applied a hammerlock. Oliver screamed like a girl, startling Kendy so much he let go.

Oliver had complained to the senior counselor, who took Kendy aside. "The kid's father is some sort of space scientist, his mother a Senator's daughter. Don't let him get away with anything, enforce the rules, but don't leave a mark on him."

Each morning, Kendy harassed Oliver to make his cot. Oliver would then run outside and harass another kid who was unable to defend himself. Oliver mastered the sly kick and the innocent denial. Kendy tried to mobilize opinion in the tent against Oliver's bullying, but others seemed unconcerned. When Oliver deliberately stood up in the war canoe, Kendy fined him a week's desserts. Then in the mess hall, Oliver refused to eat anything and spread a rumor that the food was poisoned.

One day when alone together, Kendy offered to shake hands and start over. Oliver spat on Kendy's outstretched hand. Nearly bursting with rage, Kendy had wiped his hand on Oliver's face. Oliver clamped his teeth on Kendy's finger. Kneeing Oliver, Kendy writhed free to attempt an orderly withdrawal, but Oliver followed with sharp kicks and ineffectual karate chops.

"You stinking bully, I'll Veet-cong you," said Oliver.

In defense, Kendy had hurled the kid against a tent pole, mashing his nose. Snorting blood and crying, Oliver opened his Boy Scout knife. "I'll drive you out of here if it takes a hundred years."

Kendy had grabbed his wrist and taken the knife away. He didn't report the incident because Oliver would have been expelled. But the next morning, Kendy was fired for leaving a mark on a camper. Oliver, nose swathed in tape, snuck up behind Kendy as he packed, saying tearfully, "You big bully, I'll get you if it's the last thing I ever do."

T he infrared dispenser disgorged a bubbling cheese sandwich. Kendy's mother was digging into chocolate pie heaped with whipped cream, while Mr. Smith grinned like a shrewd farm boy who had put out salt for a cow to catch the calf.

"Kendy will have an opportunity to travel the world," he said.

Kendy's mother dropped her fork. "I thought you said he'd be protected from the draft."

"Oh... he will. This would be as an exchange student."

"As a State Department Cadet?" Kendy asked.

"Possibly." Mr. Smith reached his gloved hand for the sugar. "There are other—ahem—opportunities in civilian government, with more future for young men than the State Department." He smiled at Kendy's mother. "Big organizations grow bigger. The biggest is our government. Who can foresee all opportunities for a young man to grow?"

"The pie was very good," she said, looking around and frowning.

"During his first two years at NU, he'll enjoy a broad general education." Mr. Smith handed her a dish of chilled melon balls. "We're rebuilding a citizenry with a renewed understanding of our national purpose." He looked straight at Kendy. "We're building opportunities for those few young men with intelligence and courage to shape our future."

Cornball, Kendy thought. But someone would have to, and he hoped that wouldn't be Oliver. But while NU might be big enough for them both, he didn't want to go here. He decided he'd be happier back in high school for Senior year.

"How would you straighten things out?" Mr. Smith asked.

Shocked by the question directed at him, Kendy chewed and swallowed hard. "I guess I'd like to try—in the State Department—or diplomatic service—to maintain communication between us and Russia."

"Good for you!" his mother said, getting him off the hook. "You can get an even broader education at Harvard. That's where nearly everyone in the State Department comes from anyway. Remember that nice letter you got from the registrar? When you're a Senior, they'll—"

"Mother!" Kendy blurted.

Mr. Smith replied calmly, "Yes, I heard that Harvard is a fairly good college. Because you're only sixteen, you could go there for two years. That is, until you're called out for your two years of Universal National Service, to plant trees in the mornings and study patriotism in the afternoons. Assuming your lucky number wouldn't come up for the draft."

Kendy looked away, his ears burning. Defiantly, he thought maybe he'd just volunteer with the Green Berets. Yet Congress had decreed that two years' attendance at NU would meet Universal National Service requirements.

"I'm going to level with you," Mr. Smith said. "National University is tougher than Harvard, and you're only sixteen years old."

"There are younger kids than that here," Kendy muttered, thinking of Oliver.

"You think you can hack it here? The only kids who do are brilliant young men with great maturity, patriotism, and *esprit de corps.*" Mr. Smith stood up, and Kendy felt his resolve slip away.

Mr. Smith's hand closed on his shoulder. "Let me show you our squadroom—'the barn.' There are ten guys on our team. I'd be your advisor if you want me." He smiled at Kendy's mother. "Excuse us for about ten minutes," he apologized. "Down where we're going is man's country."

Cornball, Kendy thought. Yet he couldn't help responding to Mr. Smith and couldn't quite understand why.

Their elevator plunged to the minus-seven level. From there, a metal bridge led over a court below where a shouting group of boys played full-court basketball. Kendy caught whiffs of chlorine from a pool somewhere as they walked down a hallway with dazzling artificial daylight. Widely spaced doors were numbered.

"Squadroom Nine is ours." Mr. Smith then commanded, "Nine! Nine!"

The door opened itself into a small living area where a burr-headed kid watched television. Seeing Mr. Smith, the boy acrobatically yanked both feet off the coffee table and launched himself erect.

"Hi! Sir, you're back just in time to help me with my calc."

"Then start doing it," Mr. Smith suggested, taking a backhanded swipe at him.

The kid ducked, laughing. Kendy realized the boy liked Mr. Smith. After introducing them at the door, Mr. Smith said seriously, "Kendy will add life to our basketball team."

While grinning at the compliment, Kendy was pushed lightly by Mr. Smith into the squadroom. He squinted at its artificial daylight ceiling with images of drifting clouds.

Were stratocumulus clouds also forming in the real sky seven levels above?

He guessed this ceiling worked like that commercially suppressed television his high school chem class had tried. It had had organic liquid crystals sandwiched between panes of glass coated with a transparent conductor. The backside of the glass had inductors attached to a maze of wires that converged into an electro-optical converter box. When plugged into a video tape player, a dim American flag had waved inside that glass sandwich as if it were a flat television tube. When the venetian blinds in the room were raised to let more light in, the flag had brightened.

Here, instead, was a TV camera on the roof aimed at the sky? Or perhaps instead a video tape player was connected to an electro-optical converter. Maybe it transmitted positive and negative charges, from a moving videotape to induction points hidden above this giant glass sandwich in the ceiling. To create drifting clouds, Kendy guessed that fluctuating electrical currents caused turbulence within liquid crystals, varying opacity.

"One big living room," Mr. Smith said, "helps all ten guys be good friends. More privacy than you'd have in the Army."

Kendy saw entrances to stalls connected to the living area—five on each side of the grass-green carpet.

"This would be yours," Mr. Smith said while leading him to a small room with mahogany-colored plywood walls. A sawdust-colored carpet felt springy beneath Kendy's feet. Along one wall, wardrobe closets and built-in drawers could hold everything he owned. The stall was the size of a typical college double room yet seemed crowded. It was dominated by an electrically adjustable bed which hummed when Kendy pushed the HEAD-UP button causing the pillow support to tilt up. The bed's high redwood frame held adjustable shelves, overhead tensor lamps, a swing-out writing board, and a snack-box. The room also had a television and a cartridge stereo with earphones for slumber learning.

"With your long arms, you can rearrange all this built-in bedside junk to reach everything without moving your butt."

Mr. Smith's gloved hand reached into the bed's adjustable frame and twisted a rheostat. Kendy's vision dimmed, and high in the ceiling appeared a rectangle of dark artificial sky, with Venus and other stars. Curtains crept across the front of the stall. Mr. Smith yawned and opened a little door in its rear wall.

"Here's your private study cell." It had dark plywood walls and a low ceiling.

Kendy instinctively ducked his head. The study room seemed small yet contained a dark vinyl couch and a matching chair, facing an educational console twice the size he'd seen at UCLA. Four graduate students had shared that console. This one gleamed with fascinating gadgets, including an attached helmet and wristbands.

"You can be your own best teacher. Be ten years before Harvard students get anything like this," Mr. Smith said. He opened a cabinet above the couch, revealing a mini-refrigerator and a two-burner electric stove, with a pull-out counter underneath. Next to it was a small sink with a built-in coffee brewer.

"Here's your meditation room," Mr. Smith said, turning to the opposite wall and sliding open a narrow door. "The throne is comfortable, but these bathtubs are too short for stretched-out creative thinking. I'll show you my suite. I rate a six-foot tub."

IV

From Kendy's dim stall, they walked beneath the late afternoon sky in the squadroom ceiling to a paneled conference room at the far end.

"I referee in here," Mr. Smith said. He slapped the back of his mahogany captain's chair in passing the only chair at the round table on which an aging banana peel sprawled like a brown octopus among candy wrappers. The other chairs were stacked in a corner, swapped for upholstered seminar couches which were rumpled from use. The mess looked funny in such an expensive building.

Mr. Smith unlocked the door to his own suite. Smiling, he gestured Kendy ahead into a paneled living room with a fieldstone fireplace. In an artificial picture window, birds fluttered around an iceberg. Motioning to a bearskin rug, Mr. Smith said happily, "I shot this with my little old M-16," poking the polar bear's open jaws with his wide brown shoe. That shoe appeared oddly short, as if he lacked toes. "Had to feed him a whole clip. And here's the dinette kitchenette."

Kendy stared at a wall-mounted, reddish fish resembling a salmon.

"Arctic char." Mr. Smith explained. "When the rivers thaw, they'll rise to a fast-moving Silver Doctor fly." Mr. Smith said. "When I was starving, I caught a bigger char on ermine guts and a #4 hook, but that was in Siberia. I guess you've deduced that I'm not the intellectual type. Maybe we advisers are supposed to counterbalance your professors." He opened a door. "I junked the government-issued furniture in this bedroom and built my own. Check out this homey touch."

The circular bed revolved. "Made it myself," Mr. Smith continued proudly. Kendy stared at a languorous painting of a woman on the wall.

Since kindergarten, Kendy had been exposed to pregnant rabbits and see-through plastic ladies. He'd attended "Growth" lectures and "Understanding Your Emotions" courses, and even a "Marriage and Your Future Family" series. While his technical knowledge of female anatomy was impeccable, his imagination drove him crazy. "That's—uh—a pretty good painting."

"Can't bring girls into the squadroom," Mr. Smith said, as if reading his mind and flattering him. "I'm not kidding. We must enforce congressional moral standards."

"Cars?"

"Now there's the magic word. Unfortunately, not even our biggest athletic jocks are issued cars. I admit this is a recruiting disadvantage. National U is so new, with so few alumni yet scattered out into the world, few students here expect to find car keys under their pillow. You're not even allowed to keep your own car on campus until you're an Upper Division Student with at least a 3.0 grade point average."

"You're kidding?" In truth, Kendy didn't own a car yet, and was sure Mr. Smith knew it.

"The solution would be to garage your car in San Luis Obispo, where the weekend action is. During the week I make bed checks at midnight." Mr. Smith said. "But groovy guys use ingenuity. Some have even built dummies that breathe to fool me, then run off through the dark."

As he clumped back into the living room, his voice faltered. "Ken—Kendy, since I recruited you—I hope you'll sign up for my squadron. I'm not trying to con you. You can get a good education here, and your country does need you. I'm not trying to set the hook in you."

Mr. Smith's face appeared almost twentyish, both eager and worried, as if he were once again a young—whatever he had been.

"We want you. Listen, you can learn here whatever you really want to learn." He grinned. "Congress tells us to teach patriotism, but that's something you've got to learn for yourself. Alright, let's get back to your mother."

In the coffee-teria, Kendy's mother stood hastily. "You've seen everything by now, I suppose. Are you sure you want to—"

"Of course I'm sure," Kendy interrupted, although he hadn't been sure at all. He had intended to think it over. But he told her firmly "Here's where I want to go to college."

F lying home on the commercial jet from San Luis Obispo to Los Angeles Off-Shore Airport, she asked him, "You're not making Mr. Smith another father image, like you did your jayvee basketball coach…right?"

Kendy glared at her and barely spoke during the interminable landing pattern. Then he felt choked up, helping her into the periscopic stairway as if she were a little old lady. She's almost forty, he thought, with her remaining years dwindling away. He felt both protective and trapped. Trying to help her into the cab, he toppled in behind her.

"You can let go of my apron strings," she remarked, lighting a cigarette. "If this is the big split, I'm proud of you." She put her arms around him. "You'll make some girl a good husband." She laughed. "Don't let her, or anyone, con you any worse than these stinkers already are doing."

"Who's conning me?" he asked.

"Oh, my, you don't know after today?"

He didn't want to know. Mentally he was packing his bags.

In their apartment, she looked up into his face. "And you don't even remember your father," she cried.

"I do," he muttered, wishing he did. "Nobody's going to con me," he blurted, unsure whether he meant Mr. Smith or her.

He escaped to his bedroom and tried to read the newspaper.

I n West Virginia, the rebuilding of Tin Woodman was held up by a wildcat strike. The FBI was investigating. Kendy shined his shoes on the *Los Angeles Times* editorial page, which complained that the Soviet Union was interfering with our right to explore the Moon. Their crawlers had blocked an American geological survey team outside the crater where the Soviet's vinyl dome was inflated. After being pumped full of congealing bubblets, the Soviets had failed to coat it with the usual aluminum reflectant—so would the dome house some sort of broadcasting aerial? He switched on the bathroom television to Multi-News, where he saw the gray-ish dome under surveillance from the US telesatellites.

The Soviets were chopping extra headroom within the dome, pushing out masses of bubblets from the airlock. They were carrying equipment, yet that seemed more suited for hard rock-drilling than broadcasting. The television stream showed a manned rocket arriving, then disgorging a seemingly important person as others in space suits clustered about him.

Meanwhile, in the United States, the latest unmanned Mars rocket ruptured itself during a static test. Reportedly, it had been reprogrammed to attach itself to Phobos, as had the unsuccessful *Lotka II*, hopefully to shuttle its landing module down to Mars. The Board of Inquiry suspected sabotage.

S aying goodbye at Los Angeles Off-Shore Airport, Kendy hugged his mother.

"Stay cool," her voice choked. "Don't let them con you. Stay free."

In the jet, he tried to lose his emotions among the *Los Angeles Times* pages. Significantly, the Soviet dynamiter of Tin Woodman had been exchanged for an American tourist who had been convicted of a currency violation in Leningrad. Were the Soviets, muffled and gagged within their own security procedures, using dynamite instead of words? Tin Woodman was dynamited again.

On the bus from San Luis Obispo to NU, Kendy felt more concerned with his own problems, afraid that Oliver would deliberately make trouble for him. But he grinned with excitement when finally standing among the tile-roofed buildings. He had a feeling of freedom.

Seven levels below, when Kendy lugged his suitcase into Squadroom Nine, Mr. Smith yelled with pleasure. "I have your class registration cards. Come on back to the conference room."

"I've studied the catalog," Kendy said, "and have a pretty good idea of what I want to take." Optimistically he laid his list on the table.

"Good choices," said Mr. Smith. "But Russian is a better choice than Spanish. I don't want to pressure you, but as your advisor—" Both reached for the catalog, but Kendy's hand was quicker. "Sir, I need only one more year of Spanish to—"

"You'll need more than one foreign language," Mr. Smith interrupted, "if you really want to be a diplomat."

He awkwardly placed a gloved hand on Kendy's shoulder. "You'd better start studying Russian, from the inside. For example, the word *mir* means world, but also can mean the pre-Revolution village and its decision-making method, where peasants discussed a problem until the village elder announced a unanimous decision. Ones who didn't conform became outcasts. But *mir* also means more than village commune or the world.

"Also, the Russian word for peace may have different connotations and implications in a Russian diplomat's mind than our own. One man's peace may be another man's poison. *Paz, paix?*"

Kendy's head spun. "Peace in Spanish and French, I guess," he muttered, knowing full well this conversation had become an arm-twister to make him sign up for Russian.

Mr. Smith nodded firmly. "You'll also be immersed in a Russian living experience for two hours a day, to get beneath the surface of the language. Now that's settled, let's consider the rest of your class schedule."

The advisor had written down six course titles.

Kendy's mouth was agape. No! On his own list was Spanish IV, not Russian. He wanted Biochemistry, not Calculus. And Physiology, not Physics! Worst of all, instead of Political Science and Basketball, the adviser had written down Military Science Tactics and Unarmed Combat. Only American Aspirations, a required course, was on both of their lists.

Before he'd left home, his mother had looked over his shoulder at the catalog, saying NU must be returning to the Dark Ages. Instead of offering one or two big unified experimental courses per semester like other universities, NU expected students to sign up for five or six related courses, like back in the 1960s when she was in school. She said Kendy's list of courses seemed ridiculously old-fashioned. If she had seen Mr. Smith's list, she would have squawked with rage and dissent.

"Why Unarmed Combat, not Basketball?" Kendy blurted.

"You already look good as a basketball player." Mr. Smith explained soothingly. "Only Varsity players we've recruited can enroll in Basketball for credit. You'll help us on our intramural dorm team."

"I didn't realize I was trying to sign up for Varsity," Kendy murmured, embarrassed. "But why Unarmed Combat?"

"National University students are excused from the draft only because it's understood they'll take Military Science and Tactics, plus a physical education course such as Unarmed Combat."

Kendy considered standing up and going home, but he'd told all his high school friends he's been accepted at National University.

"Integral Calculus is a necessary foundation stone for any science today." Mr. Smith's gloved finger descended on Biochemistry, blotting it out.

"But I was in the Biochem Club," Kendy protested. "That's where the future is, in the sciences."

"OK, fair enough," Mr. Smith smoothly. Kendy suspected he was being handed a little preplanned victory in exchange for something else. "Scratch Physiology off your list, and I'll scratch Physics off of mine."

"That's giving me the double shuffle," Kendy retorted, standing up, deciding to go home. His voice rose angrily. "Where's the broad general education you talked about?"

Instinctively, he hoped to enrage Mr. Smith enough to kick him out. Unless Mr. Smith laughed—then Kendy could get angry enough himself to break free. But Mr. Smith only peered up at him with a hurt expression.

"Ken—Kendy, you *will* get a broad general education. In my American Aspirations seminar, the eleven of us meet daily, discussing our futures. I'm here to advise you—for your own country. Your country needs help. Don't ask what your country can do for you."

V

After Kendy reluctantly signed all six registration cards, with only one class he'd wanted, he wearily unpacked, then met the other nine boys in Squadroom Nine. But this was the last week Mr. Smith would con him. He didn't know which squadroom Oliver was in. But later that night, in the coffee-teria, he saw Oliver's pale face. Clutching their trays, they drifted in opposite directions as cautiously as two scorpions in a very large bottle.

Unfortunately, Oliver's squadroom was located on this same minus Seventh Level. Six times a day they passed each other in the hall without speaking. Often Oliver was trotting to keep up with a huge blonde boy sporting a military crewcut and razor-nicked chin.

Meanwhile, Kendy became enamored of one girl about 19 years old who he saw regularly from a distance. She was the teaching assistant in charge of their Biochem lab section, but he didn't follow her around. She quietly tried to maintain order. But Oliver was in the same lab section. Kendy overheard him noisily attempting to show superior knowledge of "adenine-thymine nine base pairs, which ratify the double helices is of a rat's genes."

Kendy was pleasantly surprised to be elected representative for his squadron. Five of his squad mates were college Sophomores and for some reason, none of them wanted the job. Every Thursday night, as Representative, he had to attend the Seventh-Level meeting.

At Kendy's first meeting, he saw that the Seventh-Level President was Rog, the huge blonde boy with stubble on his head and shaving scrapes on his chin from Oliver's squadron. Rog was in training for the State Department.

Various dorm reps stood to offer complaints or suggestions, one finally mumbling about saltpeter. He blurted that his constituents wanted an investigation of the cafeteria food.

Rob banged his gavel. "What's more important is for Seventh Level to get revenge for last year. I want each rep to go back to his squad room and find out which guys got letters in basketball in high school. I need all of them on the court in their shorts in one hour to try out for our intramural team. Now let's hear a motion to adjourn this meeting."

Although Kendy lacked a Varsity letter, he couldn't resist watching the intramural basketball practice from the bridge above the court. Rog lumbered out on the floor with an orange ball and tin whistle, with Oliver trotting behind. Carrying a clipboard, Oliver chattered excitedly.

"Where are all my men?" Rog shouted.

Eight men finally straggled onto the court, enough for two practice teams by the new college rules. The four-man team rule was intended to reduce congestion under the baskets to make the game less of a contact sport.

Rog ran them through a layup drill. Some of the players took off on the wrong foot. When they started practicing three-point set-shots from the outside, Kendy thought the lighting must be bothering them.

When Rog tried to referee them in a practice game, some fought for rebounds after missed free shots, using high school rules. Others protested that in college the foul shooter could take the ball out of bounds after his free shot, whether he made it or not. That frequently revised college rule supposedly discouraged intentional fouling and could speed up the game. The players ran increasingly slower; all seemed out of shape.

Ignoring Oliver, Kendy wandered down beside the court, fascinated by the ineffectual and missed layups. He thought the players must have won their letters in extremely small high schools. When Rog finally allowed the wheezing sufferers to depart, the sweaty ball rolled toward Kendy.

He knew what he wanted to do, but he was hesitant at first. Finally, he ignored Oliver's glare and did it! Dribbling smoothly and flexibly toward the basket, he tried a relaxed right-hand layup, softly off the backboard and in. Warming up, he dribbled faster, his long leg muscles loosening until he felt light-footed as a grasshopper again. He tried a left-hand lay-up. Beautiful!

As Rog was leaving, Kendy raced around into a dribble-drive toward the right side of the backboard. With a fierce gasp, he leapt high, stretched higher, then slammed the ball down through the hoop in a right-hand dunk shot that banged his little finger against the iron rim. Dropping from the air triumphantly, he barely felt the pain.

"Where'd you letter?" Rog demanded. "You look better than those farmers."

Oliver stared with obvious hatred.

"You're my new Forward," Rog said, ignoring Oliver. "Let's hit the showers." Oliver was left standing.

When they came out of the locker room, Oliver scrambled down the staircase from the Seventh Level, breathing hard as if he'd run back to his room. "Rog, I have the rest of that good pie, in my mini-fridge."

"We'll go up to the coffee-teria, so Kendy can come along."

Rog ambled to the elevator, talking to Kendy. Oliver trotted behind, chattering desperately.

In the meal room, cleanup men were turning off the lights, but Rog laughed at them and handed Kendy a three-flavored sundae from the machine. The two kidded around. Kendy had learned how to get along with football jocks in high school, where most had supported his unsuccessful election campaign. Rog didn't seem too different.

Oliver shut up, gave up, and left. Kendy felt malicious triumph. Yet while Kendy got Rog another round of Cokes, who was laughing while chasing away the janitor trying to turn off the last light, Oliver reappeared. His pale face seemed even narrower from rage.

"This—Frosh—" he turned his sharp face to Kendy. "He says he's a better shot than you."

"He is." Rog laughed, crushing his paper cup into a ball but missing his one-hand set shot at the Coke machine.

"Not with a gun," Oliver said.

"Yeah, I'm also captain of the rifle team." Rog grinned at Kendy. He fired an imaginary submachine gun.

Oliver tried again. "You haven't seen the little Czech model 81 they added to the collection."

"Uh-huh." Rog reloaded his invisible submachine gun. "What are you trying to pull this time?"

"It's a really cute little fire-spitter." Oliver's voice rose uncontrollably. "Even loaded with the twenty-shot magazine, it weighs only four pounds because it fires caseless ammo, electrically ignited. Want to see it? I have a key."

"You say!" Rog lowered his voice.

"Kendy, or whatever your name is," Oliver said, "why don't you go to bed?"

"Okay," Kendy replied cautiously, preferring bed to trouble.

Unexpectedly Rog draped a heavy arm around him. "Come with us, Kendy. If this little spook can really open the Trophy Room, you'll want to see those crazy contraptions someone took from the KGB. Come with us."

Kendy grinned defiantly at Oliver.

The gym hallway was empty. The grillwork door was locked, as was an inner steel door, so they couldn't see into the Trophy Room. To Kendy's surprise, Oliver put on black silk gloves. Deftly as a surgeon, he inserted the key, turned the lock, and spread apart the grill doors. He leaned inward to unlock the inner door, using the same key.

Kendy worried there might be an alarm system. Yet no alarm sounded. Oliver pocketed the key, and Kendy realized it was a simple back-door key that any shrewd kid with a file could shape. Kendy blinked at the darkness. It didn't seem reasonable for this Trophy Room to be so easy to break into, with all these students nearby. An attractive hazard. He couldn't understand it.

Rog yanked Kendy inside. Oliver slid the jaw-like doors together, then pointed a glowing penlight he held between curled fingers. Kendy put his hands in his pockets, afraid to touch anything and leave fingerprints.

Rog slapped one big hand onto a glass-topped case, then reached behind it. "Yeah! This model 81 has an image-intensifier." Rog looked through the sight of the gun at Kendy. "Man, I can really see you through the tube! Your forehead is sweating."

Kendy shifted uncomfortably. Was it loaded?

"Got something better for you," Oliver said ominously. He had put the penlight down and now held a shiny double wand entangled in wires. It scissored like an obstetrician's forceps but was longer and its tips were different.

"You act like you're afraid of guns," Oliver remarked, moving toward Kendy.

"No," Kendy protested.

"Catch," said Oliver, tossing the gleaming crossed wands with trailing wires straight at Kendy's face.

Kendy flinched, catching them mid-air so the metal rods wouldn't strike the floor with a loud noise.

"Hold the insulated handles, stupid," Oliver said. "Do you want to get electrocuted or something?"

Oliver scurried toward Kendy and hooked the connected heavy battery box on Kendy's belt. "Spread the handles so the forehead contacts open wider, a little wider than my head." He then flipped a switch on the battery box, which hummed against Kendy's hip. Oliver backed away, adding, "Wait till I put on mine."

He then nervously scuttled behind the counter and dragged out another battery box, wired to his own set of gleaming forceps with insulated handles. Then his voice took a darker turn.

"I still remember, you big bully," Oliver yelled at Kendy. "You broke my nose, you SOB!" He moved toward Kendy in the semi-darkness with the spread forceps gleaming in front of him like crossed sabers. "I told you I'd get you someday. With these we're the same size. *En-garde!*"

Was he kidding? Kendy prudently retreated, holding his forceps up like a shield. "I didn't break your nose on purpose." He backed up, wanting to escape, run, pull the doors open. But he couldn't turn his back to Oliver. "You must be crazy."

"He's always kidding around, "Rog said calmly. "Teasing bigger guys because he's so little he thinks he can get away with it. If he bugs you too much, just kick him. He'll just run and complain to me. He thinks I'm his mother hen. Don't you, Oliver?"

Oliver wheezed. Was he crying? Kendy took another backward step, feeling cornered.

"What happens if your rods touch his?" Rog laughed. "Big sparks?"

"Stand and fight," Oliver declared. "Nobody will get hurt. You won't remember a thing."

"Ollie's playing like he's in the KGB," Rog said. "Like when a Russki creeps up behind a defector and clamps the contacts on his head. The defector forgets how to dress himself and like a baby has to learn to talk again. He doesn't remember anything to tell."

"Will it really do that?" Kendy asked, embarrassed by the shrillness of his own voice. Was this a practical joke? He didn't like being laughed at.

"Depends on the voltage." Oliver laughed.

"Hey, Oliver," Rog asked, "did you really put batteries in these lobotomizers?"

Oliver lunged too quickly for Kendy's feet to move. Kendy deflected the thrust by raising the rods of his own lobotomizer, but there was no spark, so he lurched behind the glass case, his panic compounding. He suspected that Oliver's lobotomizer was operative and his was not.

"Coward," Oliver giggled.

Retreating, Kendy gripped the closed handles like a club, a caveman's lobotomizer. He felt like screaming or climbing the walls. If this were a joke and he clubbed Oliver on the head, there would be an investigation. He didn't want to be expelled.

Kendy unhooked the humming battery box from his belt and tried to think ahead.

Oliver cried. "Stand and fight, you thin-skinned bully."

Kendy edged toward the door, defensively holding the lobotomizer before him with one hand. His other hand gripped wires from which the heavy battery box dangled.

Oliver lunged, and Kendy sidestepped, swinging the battery box past Oliver's knees and around them. As the wires jerked, Kendy let go of the lobotomizer. Oliver clumped to his knees and rolled over, entangled by the wires and the battery box. Kendy lunged toward the steel inner doors, and struggling, pulled them apart. Oliver laughed as Kendy then collided with the outdoor grill, fought to open that too, then fell into the corridor.

"You bluffed him," Rog laughed, "and I liked him better than you, you little rat. Ollie, the switch on this handle…you didn't show him how to turn it on! You little sneak—" There was a loud clunk, as if Rog had dropped the lobotomizer beside Oliver.

As Kendy hurried down the corridor, he overheard Oliver say, "I have more guts than he does! I can drive him out of the university."

"Forget it, you poor little spook—and stop following me around." Rog then shouted, "Put those back in their cases. Wait! What are you doing…"

VI

K endy retreated into a restroom stall. His stomach ached. He was so angry with himself for being humiliated that he wanted to smash Oliver's nose again. "That's what he wants—to get me expelled." Like back when Oliver had goaded him before until Kendy lost that camp counselor job. But now Oliver was older and smarter.

Kendy realized that his fingerprints were in the Trophy Room on the door handles, smeared on the glass cases, and on the lobotomizer. Oliver might leave that lobotomizer broken on the floor deliberately. The security guard would find it when unlocking the Trophy Room in the morning. There would be a quick investigation.

Back when all new students enrolled, fingerprints had been taken and all were informed that National U was tough on infractions. Not only had they expelled one freshman for a lid of dope in a suitcase, they'd turned him over to San Luis Obispo deputies to be charged as a minor possessing marijuana. While held in County Jail, the federals had opened the youth's sealed juvenile records and discovered that he'd tried to use an adult's driver's license to buy a six-pack of beer. So now he was also charged with the federal offense of falsifying his application for enrollment at National University, since he'd signed that he was of good moral character.

Oliver's glove prints would be upon his own greasy finger marks, or Rog would talk too much. All three of them might be expelled together.

K endy sat until he felt better, less paranoid. Maybe he could simply do nothing. If Oliver tried to frame him, Kendy would simply tell the truth to Mr. Smith, his friend. Kendy rationalized if Oliver used his brains instead of jealousy, he'd realize a frame-up was too risky since he couldn't depend on Rog who seemed ready for a permanent split. Oliver would have to face it and might end up hating Rog more than him.

Kendy would wait it out. If nothing happened, it was best not to get involved between those two anymore. Certainly, Oliver would retain enough cool to return the guns to their proper places, or Rog would. Kendy left the restroom stall feeling considerably better, even half-smiling at some defiantly funny graffiti.

But as he entered the hallway and looked back toward the Trophy Room, he saw a shapeless hulk. It was Rog, trying to crawl away from the Trophy Room. He was dragging his right arm and left leg as if partially paralyzed. His right arm flapped feebly at the air like an uncoordinated seal's flipper, and his face sank to the floor.

Kendy rushed to Rog and tried to hoist his bone-heavy weight to a sitting position against the wall. The doors to the Trophy Room were both closed, as if nothing had happened.

"Where's Oliver?" Kendy asked harshly.

Rog gurgled, trying to speak. His hair had a burnt smell and Kendy saw a dime-sized blister on the side of his head. The right side of Rog's face drooped.

Kendy struggled to hoist Rog's uncoordinated weight, standing Rog up on his right leg. With his shoulder under Rog's left armpit, Kendy tried to maneuver them up the hall to Rog's own squadroom and bed. Maybe he could sleep it off, and in the morning awaken as Rog again. Kenny wanted to believe that.

They only made it as far as the hall restroom. Falling from Kendy's grasp, Rog barely missed hitting his head on the basin but still hit the tile floor. Kendy winced.

Rog rolled over and sat up. He rubbed the side of his head with his good arm and peered up at Kendy. One pupil was larger than the other. "You slugged me—from behind?"

"No." Kendy wanted to leave him there. Now this mess would surely get all three of them expelled. "Don't get up," Kendy protested. "You'll fall again. I'm getting Mr. Smith." Mr. Smith would help him, cover for him, protect him like…a father. Unless he let him down…just as that jayvee basketball coach had.

The advisor lay on his back atop his round bed, asleep in his underwear with the light on. His stubby, bare feet pointed at the ceiling. One foot had a single little toe. From the other foot, all toes had been amputated.

His dresser top was in disarray, including a tipped photograph of three men grinning in furry-rimmed parkas. From the top drawer, a half-empty fifth of bourbon protruded.

"*Panidyelnik?*" Mr. Smith muttered, screening his eyes with a gray-gloved hand. "Why are you in my room?"

"Sir hi—sir!" Kendy spilled the whole story. His voice shook with fright, embarrassment, and rage.

"You don't want to be expelled." Mr. Smith closed his eyes.

"No, sir. I want to stay here, sir. Yesterday, in our American Aspirations seminar, you said one for all and all for one."

"Yeah," Mr. Smith muttered. "I guess you're the one."

He rolled off the bed and stepped across the floor to the closet. He shrugged into a faded silken black and red robe with AIR-SEA RECON 3 embroidered across the shoulders in white lettering. The robe also sported a downward-diving, red-white-and-blue dragon: wings folded beside SCUBA tanks and swim fins.

Mr. Smith laced on his special shoes. He slipped the whisky bottle from the drawer into the deep pocket of his flamboyant silk robe and grinned at himself in the mirror. "You superannuated old spook; we do the impossible."

Facing Kendy, he looked oddly young again, though his smile thinned and died. "I hope they're just putting you on for laughs."

They found Rog crawling in the hall.

"Hold it, you big poker." Mr. Smith frog-marched Rog back into the restroom and pushed him against the tile wall. "You're not faking. One pupil's dilated."

"Bed check," Rog mumbled. "Gotta go to bed."

"You slipped and hit your head on this basin," Mr. Smith said. "Drink this." From the pocket of his robe, he drew out the bottle, twisted out the cork, then squeezed Rog's throat so that his mouth opened. Mr. Smith poured in bourbon in while Rog gagged.

"I thought you were our champion boozer?" Mr. Smith grunted. "No wonder you've been busy tonight and are half paralyzed. Stop drinking all this rock-gut. I'll pour the rest into the basin, down the tubes. You can't handle hard liquor anymore, but I won't say anything. I'll cover for you if you forget what happened. Forget it all. Don't say anything. Don't answer any questions. You're so drunk you need a medical checkup after falling and hitting your head."

Kendy didn't understand what was happening. He helped Rog as they walked down the hall to the elevator, then the dispensary, and into the isolation room.

"Lie down. Kendy, find him a hospital gown. I'll get the doctor."

Eventually Mr. Smith returned with the doctor. By then, Rog could control his right arm fairly well. During the encephalographic examination, his pupils began to equalize. The doctor said he might have suffered a concussion— to keep him under observation for twenty-four hours. He added, "Also, young man, stop this drinking before it's too late."

Mr. Smith grinned. "Rog, you know you could be expelled for boozing in a federal dormitory. We'll keep our mouths shut. You do the same."

The clock indicated 2:42 AM. Kendy felt dizzy with weariness. He hoped Rog would be all right.

Mr. Smith shrugged. "Let's go for a walk. You know where?"

"Do you think he's still in there?" Kendy mumbled when they stood in front of the grillwork door to the Trophy Room. "It's locked."

"Do you want a key?" Mr. Smith left. "It hangs in plain sight in the building superintendent's office, with a concealed camera aimed at it from the ceiling. I won't steal it for you, though. I don't want to lose my pension."

"It's a trap," Kendy muttered. A simple key hung in plain sight had been an invitation to copy it. "Got to find Oliver and take his key away from him."

"If he's not inside," Mr. Smith said softly, hooking his gray fingers in the grill work door to the Trophy Room.

"My fingerprints are inside."

Mr. Smith smiled, looking at the ceiling. Was there a hidden surveillance lens? If so, at any moment the night security guard might look down this hall and catch them. But Kendy saw no lens. In the waste basket on the floor, Kendy groped through paper cups and candy wrappers and found the key.

"You just improved your grade," said Mr. Smith, acting not at all surprised.

Kendy used his handkerchief to hold the key unlocking both Trophy Room doors. Mr. Smith grinned inanely and clumped straight across the dark room to the light switch.

On top of the glass case lay the Czech Model 81 submachine gun which Rog had played with. Kendy stared at both lobotomizers on the floor, one nearer the door. No Oliver. Beside Kendy's foot gleamed droplets of blood. Perhaps Oliver had ended up with a bloody nose.

"That crazy little idiot," muttered Kendy. "I can't understand why he would attack Rog. I thought he hated me."

Frantically, Kendy wiped off the lobotomizer his prints were on. "Maybe Oliver is still in the building, getting the security guard. Maybe he's set a trap for me."

Mr. Smith had closed the steel doors and was casually polishing the glass cases with the sleeve of his robe. "If you luck out of this without being expelled, you'll be older, maybe wiser. But in five years I'm expecting my full pension. I could blow it all for helping you. You know this is federal property. Breaking in here is a federal offense."

Mr. Smith abruptly returned the gun to its glass case. "I'd be nuts to help you after spending my whole life, since age seventeen, serving my country. Two undeclared wars, wounded twice. I've *earned* that pension. Ever heard of Vorkuta? It was cold up there!

"I was there two whole years before being exchanged for a covert Soviet secret agent. That agent in Boston had been caught with his arm in a hollow tree, attempting to retrieve microfilm. But it had already been removed from that drop. Glorious exchange! I came back to the United States, albeit with missing digits." He sighed. "Let's get out of here."

Kendy realized Mr. Smith had been put out to pasture at National U. At that moment, he felt sorry for him. Mr. Smith's placed a gloved hand on Kendy's shoulder, shoving him gently toward the door. Quietly they slipped out of the Trophy Room.

"Lock the doors," Mr. Smith whispered. "Start worrying about the key."

Kendy was dizzy with weariness. "What to do… about Oliver?" He thought he should dispose of the key, not hide it.

Mr. Smith was muttering, "… a serious talk about your future."

VIII

B learily, he followed Mr. Smith through the sleeping darkness of Squadron Nine. They shuffled across the grass-like carpet beneath the glittering stars and into the conference room. From across the mahogany table, Mr. Smith pushed a cup of coffee toward Kendy.

Kendy shook his head yet felt grateful for Mr. Smith's help.

Mr. Smith's aging face peered through the steam rising from his own coffee cup. "I need you to do something for me."

"Gee, yes." In that moment of sleepy gratitude, Kendy would've done anything for him as if... *Father, father!*

"Next year, enroll as a freshman at USC."

"What? What?" Kendy's voice broke in disbelief and anguish. "You don't want me here?"

"Don't look like that. You can come back here after two years. We'll send your scholastic records to the USC registrar. We'll show that you were an honor graduate from an exclusive prep school we subsidize near Palo Alto."

His gloved hand reached across the table toward Kendy. He laughed. "On your prep school records, if you like, you can be shown as Student Body President."

"Of a nonexistent high school? What are you doing to me? First you recruited me; now you're flunking me out?"

"We need you," Mr. Smith's expression slipped between aging fright and youthful enthusiasm, "...to do two important things, while you're young enough to do them. The first is for practice. USC enjoys research contracts funded by the Defense Department, but here at National U we have the most important contract. We test security precautions at the other universities."

"You want me to infiltrate USC?" Kendy blurted, his leg muscles tightening. "Like a spy. Was this the plan all along? Wait—how did Oliver get that key?" He stood up, angrily.

"Sit down. You'll simply have one easy security problem to complete during your first year, to continue earning your tuition. But you have a bigger problem than switching schools.

"You're one of three students who broke into a federal security area, the Trophy Room. Rog is recovering from an accidental mental overload and probably will be expelled for something else. Oliver will be found, retained here, and protected, what with his parents' status. You're only sitting here because I'm protecting you."

Kendy looked at Mr. Smith suspiciously. Had he known about Kendy's history with Oliver? Played them against each other?

"I'm going home."

Mr. Smith sighed, realizing his strategy was not working.

"If you do, there will be an official investigation as to why you left. I can't protect you. I'll be arrested too unless I cooperate with my superiors. As a minor, you'd probably be remanded to the California Youth Authority security building until you're twenty-one. Then there will be a federal court trial under security conditions. Unless the National Emergency has been repealed by then, you'll probably serve 10 to 20 years as an adult."

"For what? For what?"

"Breaking laws, obviously." He shrugged. "With so many new laws, you break them by breathing. Ever since Congress declared the National Emergency, for nine years they've passed increasingly stringent laws, trying to keep the lid on. At least let me cover for you."

"You're conning me," Kendy cried, "not helping me. You waited like a vulture for me to make a mistake—maybe even orchestrated that. Waited for me to break a law. I refuse to be a spy."

"That's the wrong word." Mr. Smith's face flushed. "Not a spy. You're not qualified to be a spy. You'll simply be a Freshman, assigned to photograph a classified centrifuge, to test security procedures. You'll complete your assignment, then we'll mail the photographs to USC's Chief Security Officer. We'll explain how you penetrated their security so he can make necessary corrections."

"What if I'm caught?"

"We'll notify the FBI, and the whole thing will be hushed up. Happens every day. This is necessary if we're to maintain security in this world. What a paradox! Fortunately, those brave men you mistakenly criticize, denigrate, and mislabel as mere spies are more skilled, intelligent, and enlightened than you could ever be!"

Mr. Smith seemed genuinely angry. "Intelligence-gathering services do more to prevent war than diplomats. Intelligence agents restrain so-called statesmen from miscalculations that could kill us all. How well I know! That's why you're alive today—ungratefully sneering at spies."

"I want to be a diplomat—not a stinking spy."

This time Mr. Smith didn't get angrier. He weirdly smiled, insisting, "You'll learn. You're too honest with yourself to be a diplomat. Diplomats can't negotiate realistically with their heads twisted backwards, performing for their own people who don't know what they want. Ours talk only toward American voters. There's less genuine face-to-face communication between diplomats. In effect, they all blindly bump bottoms, reciting to please their own people."

Mr. Smith grimaced. "Believe me. It's the intelligence-gathering services who listen to what the other side really wants, what the other side is afraid of, what the other side can do. Our agents prevent miscalculations by politicians. To prevent wars and riots, honest "spies" affect the communications media, modify public opinion, and try to save us from chaos, while you wrinkle your nose at them."

"You've conned me from the day you started recruiting me."

"Well, if you believe that," Mr. Smith said, "consider it part of your education."

"You've screwed up my education from the start. You changed my class schedule until biochem was the only significant course I had."

"Become a biochemist if that's the life you want. At USC you can learn advanced lab techniques. They have recruited an old fan from overseas, who now calls himself Dr. Magadan Smyert. He was E. Vavilov's teacher."

"It's all got nothing to do with me," Kendy cried out. Yet he vaguely remembered that Dr. Smyert had escaped to America only a few weeks after Dr. E. Vavilov's return from Phobos. Dr. Smyert had claimed no knowledge of why *Lotka II* hadn't descended to Mars. He said he'd been in Leningrad, planning simple laboratory procedures for unskilled student technicians.

"Everything in the world has something to do with you." Mr. Smith. He cautiously touched Kendy's shoulder. "I've saved you from being expelled, jailed, or drafted. All I ask is a minimum of patriotism."

Kendy cried shrilly, "My mother warned me about guys like you."

"Your mother is shrewd. She's patriotic too, in her own way, but tangled in a past she remembers before the National Emergency. All the labels have changed since then. She would've been called a liberal at that time. Now she's a chaos worshiper. What does she want? A return to disorder in the streets?"

"I'll be damned if I understand what's going on now," Kendy muttered, swaying towards sleep again.

Mr. Smith helped him up. "Just as we can't understand noises from galactic space, don't know why the Russians retreated from Phobos, and don't know what they found on our Moon. They've drilled into something under that plastic dome. Maintained superb security. We can't get near E. Vavilov—yet.

"You claim it's got nothing to do with you. Listen, kid, any new knowledge is like a sharp edge of a weapon emerging. It will have a lot to do with us all."

He pushed a tottering Kendy out of the conference room, through the squad room, under the artificial stars, and across the grassy carpet toward his stall.

"A few hours sleep," Mr. Smith whispered, "and you'll know I'm right."

"Wait…" Kendy mumbled. "USC's only one. You said two missions. What's the other?"

"They didn't tell me."

Suddenly Kendy realized his first 'mission' had been planned all along, long before the Trophy Room fiasco ever happened.

He collapsed onto his bed, exhausted by empty grief and betrayal. Yet as he lay on his back, staring at his star-spangled false sky, a strange hope gradually emerged. He drifted asleep, wondering if perhaps he had a greater purpose than simply enduring National University.

When he awoke, he felt ready to face the universe, even as a spy. *His* choice.

"From now on, nobody's going to con me!"

500 POINTS FOR FATHER IMAGE

A brief tale written in Santa Barbara,
CA between 1952 and the '60s
Setting: United States on an Election Day, in the future

The President of the United States leaned forward on his folding chair in dismay, realizing what was happening out on the floodlit, flag-draped National Election Day television stage.

The collapsible metal chairs of the President's supporters creaked frantically behind his back. He heard someone say, "Look at that fat candidate waving his arms! Already 442 points. I can't look! No, wait—444 points, and he's still got two minutes to go on the big clock!"

Another voice shouted, "448 points for Father-Image. 450 points—is that a new record? Oh, now 464 points!— Mr. President, you can't possibly beat that, you've about lost this re-election!"

Metal chairs crashed, and before the President's fifth— and final—turn to speak, his supporters all deserted him. He was left alone in the Incumbent's Waiting Room.

"I can't understand it," creaked a departing voice. "464 points for Father-Image, and the candidate's not even married. He's wearing a pink bowtie, yet!"

Onstage, the Candidate spoke hurriedly, his pudgy fingers spread. "Four score and seven years ago, old soldiers never die. We have nothing to fear but fear itself. I shall return, two chickens in every pot."

On the Big Scoreboard, ablaze with giant cigarettes and canned orange juice advertisements, the red-thermometer line of the candidate's Father-Image category crept up to an insurmountable 469, then, for no reason at all, edged to 470.

"Prosperity is just around the corner! I shall go to Korea! Beware of foreign entanglements. We shall open a new frontier." His score jumped to 478.

The President nervously lit a cigarette. Not one, but two points for each of his competitor's last four Father-Images? Those tested electoral phrases had been used by every successful candidate since before Quebec was admitted as the 59th State and were never worth more than one point each.

"Fifty-four forty or fight!" The Candidate hurried through his last minute. "Fifty miles before breakfast. I believe in Dick. We hold these truths to be self-evident."

The President still sat alone in the Incumbent's Waiting Room. His cigarette smoke made him ill. He searched for an ashtray. What a way to lose an election! "Damn that Dr. Gallroper!"

A man in sagging trousers sauntered into the room and slowly handed him an ashtray.

"Mistah, dat's who he's imitatin' out der, wid duh bow-tie and duh stupid grin. Like you say, dat's like Dr. Gallroper."

He ran his hand through uncombed hair. His mouth sagged, then he said, "I got a long memory back to when dis machinery was screwed in. Dr. Gallroper, dat's who, wid da bowtie, screwing it in. Dis Candidate's not so fat as Dr. Gallroper, but he looks like him. No wonder dis guy's makin' a big score for Father-Image."

"Dr. Gallroper was a great man," the President said severely. As an acne-scarred high school Student Body President in the 1960s, he'd cut his political teeth on Dr. Nielsen S. Gallroper's definitive text: *Digging the Bedrock of Voter Motivation in an Age of Total Communication.*

Yet as a thin young City Councilman, he'd scowled his way through Gallroper's *Liberating Public Opinion Sampling from the Fickle*. It had seemed vaguely immoral. Later, as triumphant City Mayor, he'd shrugged at Gallroper's *Five Subconscious Motivants of Voter Behavior.* That one was for the psychiatrist's couch, not for practical politicians.

When he had been overwhelmingly defeated in his bid for election to the United States Senate, he'd had more time to read (and narrow-eyed, study) Gallroper's axe-grinding new book: *An Efficient Electoral Process Based on Electronic Integrity.* He'd thrown that one on the floor. The old man's earlier works had merit, but he'd gotten senile.

Sponsored by a trio of great electronic corporations, Dr. Gallroper appeared nightly on television, enthusiastically repeating his famous speech: "Instantaneous Democracy, a Voting Machine Attached to Every Television Set." But that concept never got off the ground. No one would pay the electronic installation charge of $488 per set just for the right to vote.

Without a sponsor, Dr. Gallroper was reduced to printing and distributing a thin pamphlet with the teaser: "How poor taxpayers can save time and money and even make a profit, on election day!"

The President rubbed his stinging eyes in remembrance. It was that thrifty tide of voters who had swept him to governorship with praises of Gallroper on his lips. In his pocket, he'd tucked the doctor's earlier work on subconscious movitants of voter behavior—despite his former opinion about that being psychobabble.

After his governorship, when running for President, he had learned enough from Dr. Gallroper to set a new record for Father-Image at 450 points, while scoring strongly in the other categories. That was four years ago. After the President's Inaugural Address, Dr. Gallroper had waddled toward him, grinning, decrepit with age. He had shaken his hand—then vanished.

A warning buzzer sounded from the big scoreboard and floodlights dimmed slightly. The opposing Candidate concluded his speech with a sweep of his fat hand, "Marconi thanks you, Falla thanks you, all of my pets thank you," and his Father-Image rose to an incredible 493 out of 500.

Bells rang, bugles sounded, and giant images of cigarettes emitted puffs of smoke as the Candidate waddled triumphantly from the stage.

The President realized the janitor was still in the room with him.

"I turn it on in the mornin'." The janitor leaned heavily on his push broom. "I dust ut real careful and turn ut off, put ut to bed at night." He hitched uselessly at his sagging trousers. "But I don't unnerstan' that machine. Dr. Gallroper never looked like no Father-Image to me."

The President hurled his pack of sponsor-issued cigarettes to the floor and stood up.

"Hey, where yuh goin', Mister?"

The President strode onto the stage for that final category. He automatically turned the giant can of orange juice, so his name appeared below the sponsor's. But the television cameras had turned away from him—as if the election were already over, a foregone conclusion. Everyone was focused on the Big Scoreboard.

The President's lips narrowed with determination. Mathematical figures do not lie. Scores were arranged in irrefutable neon columns. He needed an impossible 494 points in the final category to tie. That would throw the election decision into the House of Representatives: a momentous event that had only happened once.

CATEGORY	CANDIDATE	INCUMBENT
1. Youthfulness	462	390
2. Humility	375	415
3. Generosity	432	402
4. Alertness	406	467
	(1,675)	(1,674)
5. Father-Image	493	
	(2168)	

To win, he needed 495 points. In the last election, his record for the Father-Image had been only 450. It was obvious he'd been licked.

Already the audience was already switching channels to the exciting images and sounds of Roller Derby. Nevertheless, the Introduction Trumpet sounded, and the gleaming eyes of the television camera zoomed in on him. A bell rang. The Big Scoreboard allotted him the customary 200 points—just for putting in an appearance.

"Friends, four years ago I spoke of my wife." His Father-Image score rose to 210. "I spoke of my nine children." 219. "Of my twenty grandchildren." 239. "Now I have thirty-eight grandchildren." The score rose to 277, then jiggled uncertainly. The machine realized its erroneous interpretation, synching back to the arithmetically correct 257.

"At the beginning of this program tonight, I appeared before you to be rated for Usefulness. I told you of my plans for the future." The president spoke as if the Big Scoreboard were not between them.

"In the following round, when my worthy opponent and I were graded for Humility, I explained my four-year record in office." The President pointed at the scoreboard. "Compare our Humility scores—an important category for everyone. In the third round, Generosity, you heard my opponent's vague promises of handouts. I instead guaranteed better living for us all. Surely his score is deceptive."

The President saw his Father-Image score stall at 259. An orange warning light flashed.

"Yes, it's time for an orange juice commercial, and I shall ignore it!" His voice rose, as if he could outshout the brief advertisement on tape broadcasting into his audience's living rooms.

"I shall keep speaking to the real listeners. Less than an hour ago, you rated me high above him in Alertness. In these days of hair-trigger international complications, Alertness should have special weight—worth twice as much as any other category." His Father-Image score went down four points, and he nodded somberly.

"Now, at last we are being rated for the most important quality of the four categories." The Big Scoreboard gave him back four points. "I speak of Father-Image!" His voice resounded with enthusiasm and the score jumped to 269. "But Father-Image is a fraud, a misconception!"

The Big Scoreboard buzzed and flickered. The red thermometer line for Father-Image slid all the way down to 200. He had meant to be courageous, but less emphatic.

Still, he pressed on. "I ask you, what did the learned Dr. Gallroper truly intend to measure in this category? He was a dedicated man, a very dedicated man. As a scientist he toiled for long hours, far into the night, for all of us. He built intricate banks of recognition transmitters, which work as perfectly today as when they were installed." The President's score increased by 5 points.

"But what did he intend to measure in the Father-Image category?" He pointed upward. "Sacred voter identification! The wonderful dim memories of reassurance and strength from our collective childhood.

"My not-so-worthy opponent has fouly satirized these memories. By a self-serving masquerade, he is attempting to destroy Dr. Gallroper's high hopes and expectations for the political future of our great land. He is attempting to deceive the Big Scoreboard!"

The President pointed at it. "It cannot be deceived. It knows Dr. Gallroper is dead, rest his soul, and the Big Scoreboard is greater than us all. It knows what it needs. It knows that the Presidency is greater than the sum of five categories. It is the *soul* of Big Scoreboard who will decide which man will be President."

He watched the scores expectantly, but they did not rise nor collapse. The opposing candidate's score remained at its impossibly high 463.

The Big Clock devoured time implacably.

"Father-Image isn't infallible," the President muttered. He dug his toe into the carpet, while scowling at the Big Scoreboard. For that, his Father-Image score fell ... to zero. A row of orange lights flickered on the board and the President knew he must act quickly before it cut him off the air.

He winced, then fingering his belt buckle, loosened his belt until his trousers sagged. Wearily, he also sagged his mouth open, then said, "Duh reason you shud give me the biggest score for Father-Image," he mumbled, "duh reason, dat is. What is duh reason?"

The red thermometer line rose his Father-Image score to 100, then 200, and paused.

"Duh reason is a father, he looks after his child. He takes care of him—uh—or her." Wearily, he mussed his hair, then scratched himself under the armpit. His Father-Image rose to 300. Then 400.

"Me, dat's what I do. I take care of yuh." He said, thickly, "I turn yuh on in the mornin'." 450. "I dust yuh. I turn yuh off and put yuh to bed at night," he finished, ashamed.

Suddenly the great Electoral Gong reverberated through the empty auditorium. He looked up and saw his Father-Image had reached 500. Victory! The bugles blared.

The President stood still, gasping with emotion, then straightened his tie, hoisted up his pants and tightened his belt. He had been reelected President.

He made a mental note to thank the janitor. He would find another job for him—perhaps in an embassy in Timbuctoo. Maybe even farther, Mars... As for the Big Scoreboard, the reelected President would care for that himself.

With a sledgehammer.

COUNTERATTACK

A short story written in St. Augustine, FL, 1951-52
Setting: Earth, with a strange visitor from Venus

Although he still felt queasy from deceleration effect, B.J. Plunkett dutifully fumbled into his vest pocket for an Everbreathe cigar. Vaguely he wondered if Transmutation Industries held controlling interest in Everbreathe. Quite likely. An impressive-looking cigar, its taste was impressively vile. But Public Relations would get that hang-dog look if the video-casters caught him empty-faced.

"It's your trademark," they said. "Means solid, safe, dependable—like Winston somebody or other." They had looked quite hurt the time he forgot his cigar.

"Sir!" His secretary's lighter was quicker than the captain's.

He wished they would smoke it for him too. The plush landing copter whirled them from his stateroom, high on the cigar-shaped Transmutations flagship, across the black, glassy circle of countless landing spaces to the artificial marble spaceport. He was a sick man.

Despite the swaying and lurching of Earth beneath his size-12 feet, he managed to stand relatively straight by aligning himself with one of the pillars behind the crowd. He managed a fine, toothpaste grin around his cigar. Public Relations would be proud of themselves. If I don't fall on my face, he thought.

His heart quieted a bit. He repeated his Plunkett grin for a pleader whose flashbulb had misfired. Suddenly he wanted to slap the boy on the back, give him a private interview or something. They were for him, they were his pals, good guys, all of them.

He uptilted his cigar and answered questions one at a time, with a smile in his eyes. "Yes, we have a few anthropological questions to iron out, but the Venus Refinery is a cinch to pay off."

"…No, not only for Transmutation stockholders, for the nation…

"…Yes, those alien vegetable-created men learn quickly…

"… No, except for the few incidents with our women, which some of you fellows have overplayed.

"…No, the number of lynchings has decreased. We are educating our men to let the proper authorities step in, should there be further degradations…

"…Oh, come on. The opposition planted that. How could you say my forthcoming marriage to the President's niece makes me 'heir apparent'? But I'll be grooming our sons for the race. Fine old American custom.

"Will I show up at church Sunday? Wouldn't you? Now boys, let Joe take over. I have a little fence-mending to do. He'll tell you about the squad of anthro men I'm sending. They should dope out the reason the natives have lost interest in working in our plants and have them back in no time."

As B.J.'s entourage opened a path between the newsmen, guiding him to his private copter, Joe's voice rasped after him. "Yeah, funny thing, guys, they are a lot less gruesome looking than they were a year ago. Been molding their vegetable/fish features more manlike, with a bit of human matter, so they won't offend us. They are more like us in many ways."

Ed, his general manager for Earth, lumbered at him with widespread arms. "Hello-oh-oh B.J. You happy with your vegetable men? You make us all rich, daddy?"

"Hey, cut it out. Remember my heart." B.J. laughed. "Crank her up," he shouted at the pilot. He turned to Ed, saying, "Gotta visaphone you-know-who. Here, want my cigar? No? Out the window she goes."

"Uh, B.J., could you call her from the office?"

"Uh oh. Problems?"

"No, not exactly. But your brother's waiting there to see you."

"Interesting, especially since I'm an only child."

"Well, he didn't exactly say he was your brother, but I figured it from looking at him. Thought he might be a black sheep you wanted to keep out of sight. So I put him in the Big Brass waiting room."

"Aw, Ed, he's probably just some job or contract hunter starting from the top and working down. Would you divert him to Personnel or Purchasing or any other place? You know how I hate to say no."

"O.K., but this guy is worth the price of admission. With him around you wouldn't need a mirror."

"Maybe we could train him to give after-dinner speeches and smoke big black cigars."

"Haw, that's a good one, boss. You know, this guy's a card too. Said he arrived from Venus yesterday. 'What on?' I asked him, saying 'the ship doesn't come till tomorrow.' He grins just like you do, and said, 'Oh, I came the Long Arc route. That's a day quicker.'"

"Long Arc," B.J. repeated thoughtfully. He fumbled unconsciously for another cigar. "One of our teams is nosing into that theory—traveling the opposite direction to reach any point by bending space-time. We'll eventually get there, but not yet."

They'd just taken the Short Arc of the circle to get from Venus to Earth. "Apparently some light takes the Long

Arc," Ed said, "but it's awfully tired light before it gets here. Personally, I can't see who'd want to go the long way, but some of the theory boys are all hepped up because two and two equal one out there. So I keep them happy. When they pay off, they'll pay off big."

B.J. brightened. "Mary! I'm going to marry Mary. I'll call her on the visaphone while I give my 'brother' the once over. Maybe he's a freelance theory man with something new on the Long Arcs."

Ed said, "Funny thing, my Venutian valet read a journal article on that. I asked him, just for laughs, what those Arcs were all about. I swear, he explained it a lot better than I could. Maybe their Vo-language communication permits them insights we boys can only scratch at. You know, like that Navoho, Paul Gunbow, with his teleportation theories at Yale. He claims they can only be handled using words off Navoho stems."

The express elevator whipped B.J. and his general manager to the marbled waiting room.

As B.J. shook hands with the stranger, he thought the man looked older than him, what with circles around the eyes as if he'd had a bad night. But maybe he had those eye circles too. He'd had very little rest on the space crossing. The company doc would probably not allow another.

He ushered the man, who said his name was Dick Roe, into his private office. Did he let his own stomach stick out that way? B.J. sat down in his Spine-Curve chair and offered the man a cigar. The man turned it down, saying "Got to watch my heart."

"Just make yourself comfortable, Dick, while I make a call. Then I'll hear your offer. Ed, you can go whack off a few holes of golf."

As B.J. dialed while sitting at his huge glass desk, he eyed the man's blue suit. If he hadn't known better, he could have sworn it was his own Sunday blue, the one with extra-wide lapels and lightweight sleeves.

Mary's face lunged from the blur of his visascreen.

To ease the excited pressure in his chest, B.J. almost bellowed. "Sweetheart, your boy's back. Ready for the main event?"

"You have your nerve." Mary's face, although she was fifteen years his junior, little more than a deb, was strangely dull and old. "This morning I woke up to the monstrousness of what we did last night. Only two days till Sunday and you sneak in and spoil it. Now you try to joke over as though it never happened. If I didn't love you so, I'd leave you waiting at the church."

"But I wasn't …" B.J. stopped abruptly. The man in his blue suit, who could of course hear every word although off-angle from the visascreen, was meticulously examining his fingernails.

"Listen Mary," B.J. rushed, assembling his thoughts rapidly. "I love you too much, that's my trouble. Sometimes I lose my head. I'll be right over." He flipped off the screen.

Slowly opening the side drawer, he turned his face past Dick Roe's to look in the long mirror between the progress charts. It stared back at him, wide-nostriled, wide-eyed, paler than Dick's, but otherwise identical.

The man stretched comfortably. He showed no surprise when B.J. raised his revolver above the level of the desk.

"If you think I came to blackmail you, you're mistaken," he laughed. "Nor did I come for you to righteously murder me. You won't do that, not yourself anyway, because emperors of space, big men of your ilk, do things at long range. You may work people to death or change their ways of life, until they might as well be dead. But men like you don't splatter brains on the rugs of their private offices."

His smile was infuriating.

"No," B.J. shouted, suddenly erect and flushed with rage. "I'll call the law."

"How lurid!" Dick Roe exclaimed with mock horror.

Headlines flash through B.J.'s mind. Impossible. Mary herself must never know. His heart became a drum. With a roar, he lunged around the desk with all the drive of his youth. As he fisted the gun in a savage arc, the man slipped deftly aside.

"Careful, remember your heart." The man laughed, and he smashed his fist against B.J.'s chest with unhuman force.

Gently he lowered B.J.'s corpse into the Spine-Curve chair, exchanged their clothing and credentials, then ran for the company doctor.

Big shoes I'm stepping into, he thought with a slight feeling of awe. *But more of us will come to help.*

Dick Roe, now B.J. Plunkett, moved to the window. He'd heard in the daytime they could make out Venus. He strained his eyes awhile, wishing the doctor would hurry up, for he was eager to go comfort Mary.

He needed a sun bath too. It was a long time since he had enjoyed photosynthesis.

PART TWO: TOUCHY TECHNOLOGY

I'VE GOT TO SAVE JFK

A longer story in three parts, written in
Santa Barbara, CA around 1977
Settings: Los Angeles CA and Dallas, TX in 1993 redux.

M y childhood was shattered that crazed day in 1963—
November 22nd—a grave announcement interrupted
our television program. The President had been shot in
Texas.

I didn't know what to feel. My parents huddled in front
of our black-and-white set, my father in his underwear
because he needed to sleep in the daytime. The distraught
announcer kept repeating himself. I began talking because I
wanted Mother, as she wept, to pay attention to me, to clarify
what was being said. I was home from school because smog
made my asthma worse.

I argued against that announcer. "It hasn't happened,"
I wheezed, "Look at our clock, Mom. It isn't 12:30 yet." I
was temporarily confused by time zones, then felt foolish,
since I was almost thirteen.

Father shook his head at me, as if wondering how I
could be so dumb. He stood up, saying that whatever was
happening wouldn't make any difference to us anyway.
"I still got to get to sleep so I can get up and go work the
midnight shift." He stepped aggressively toward me, wiping
his hand across his T-shirt. I backed away, determining to
do something with my life.

Two days later, on television, I saw Oswald shot, clutching his stomach.

Five days later, I watched Little John-John salute at his father's funeral procession.

I read newspapers, magazines, and a never-ending flood of books with an increasing sense of loss and bewilderment. I became part of that national obsession. But I also studied harder. I pondered a book of his speeches, which confused me.

After high school graduation, despite my difficulties with standardized tests, I managed to get into the university and survive. My asthma kept me out of Vietnam. While other students orated as if they might change America, I got into grad school. There, I learned how to apply for government grants. Deceiving four committees, I reported on Microwave Amplification by Stimulated Emission of Radiation—what I called MASERs. My boyhood dreams reached out.

Where did I hope to find myself in adulthood? In some utopia? Playing touch football on the lawn at Camelot with a 76-year-old John F. Kennedy, an elder statesman whose long life and enthusiasm gave his United States continuing courage and unity?

I hoped so. I became determined to save JFK.

1993 Dallas

Now in 1993 I have finally perfected my MASER device, to the point I can send an electromagnetic radiation spark back in time. My connected dials allow me to control how far back—within seconds. Too bad I can't time-travel myself. But I'll do my best with what I've invented so far. One small spark might change history.

Fortunately, my flight today from Los Angeles landed on time in Dallas, with my MASER undetected in my suitcase. In my rental car I drive toward Dealey Plaza, as Elm Street lunch-hour traffic roars. I park next to the high-extension rig awaiting me, thanks to my Dallas connections.

The rig sits across the street from the Texas School Book Depository, which towers like a monstrous tombstone. I unfold the building's yellowed plans.

While I measure from the corner, I sweat inside stolen coveralls too tight where I breathe.

I wish Americans a generation ago had saved his legend.

My thoughts reel like a tape recorder, playing multiple tracks as I ponder potential parallel histories. What new history might I create? My hurrying hands set up the surveying transit to sight into the sixth floor of that many-windowed brick building which had bloomed above Kennedy's motorcade thirty years ago.

So much has been written since then, national catharsis or nightmare, we've ironically lost him in a storm of words.

My big-knuckled hands grip the rig's control levers. My face sweats as I look up. I extend a long steel boom like a lengthening wand, lifting the globular tip of my invention high in the air. It's now positioned directly across from that sixth-floor window, where long ago, Oswald peered out—one eye inching inexorably toward the hard rim of his telescopic sight.

Pigeons flutter past the shiny globe at the tip of this tall rig. I clamber from its cab to drag out my other suitcase. My heart pounds as I open my case and squint at its panel of chronometers, moving toward opportunities.

With hurried strides, I unreel the rig's insulated cable to make a high-voltage connection with Dallas. I need a strong jolt of electricity for this. As a police car cruises by, I wheeze like an accordion, but from asthma, not anxiety. I'm past that. My quick-fingered hands connect the timer box to the rig. I feel exhilarated and hopeful, like a gambler entering a multi-spatial roulette game. My data is unlikely to be accurate to the exact second.

I know from history only the minute Oswald fired that fateful shot, so I twist the timer's lowest knob another three clicks to the right, three seconds farther back through thirty years into the unknown. I focus on my chronometer. It's nearing 12:30. I clamp on my headset, so I'll remember my last moments—protecting my memories in case I actually change history.

Within the seashell roar of traffic, I wait as the timer clicks through my earphones. I glance along Houston Street, where the President's gleaming limousine once glided at this very minute toward that depository.

From that high window, Oswald had a head-on view. But for some reason he hadn't taken a shot while the convertible approached the building—not even when it turned left beneath his corner window. As the car had moved away from him, it was momentarily obscured by a tree. It was then his finger began the first squeeze.

Although time offers great resistance, I'm hopeful my beam will travel back through time to just the right moment, to create a tiny epileptic spark in Oswald's brain circuitry.

As I peer up at the rig's bulbous tip, the clicking in my headphones stops. I'm blinded by a lightning implosion-explosion.

M y eyesight clears.
Fuzzily, I look at my surroundings. My first disappointing impression is that, at least in Dallas, I changed nothing. Feeling disoriented, I sleep during my flight back to LA.

Taxiing home to the university, L.A. feels off—but I can't put my finger on why. When I enter my concrete basement lab, it appears unchanged. The concrete floor is water-stained as ever. The rusty pipes on the ceiling drip. My eyes sting from ever-pervading smog. I'm still wheezing. My iron shelves are still crowded with history books. Even if I did revise the future, I must still be searching back to that era when the United States was supreme and all things seemed possible.

Yet some of my books are missing. Manchester's *The Death of the President* has vanished, as if never written. I notice several odd titles. My heart begins pounding. I stride past disturbingly similar electronic equipment on my concrete floor and unlock the iron door. I rush upward through the concrete service tunnel toward dazzling daylight, to see what I missed. Did I give America another chance?

Outside the Physics building, the sun isn't as high as it was in Dallas. Its smoggy brilliance is snagged by eucalyptus branches.

I blink at distracted faces crossing the quad between rows of parked mini-cars and suddenly realize the grass I remember is now gone. A girl nods, then smiles at me. She's so pretty I feel my face burning, but I dodge conversation. I stride to a newspaper rack to pull out the gray campus paper. Holding it at arm's length, I squint at its headlines. The small print is blurry to me. If there was change, it seems nothing changed for the better. The United States is as isolated and as threatened. People still feel helpless, and I still need bifocals.

But what happened to Kennedy? I feel terribly disillusioned. If he lived, had I saved the wrong man? Should I have set up my equipment in the Ambassador Hotel's kitchen to save his brother, instead? It seems John F. Kennedy did practically nothing with the extended life I may have given him. I feel betrayed.

"Ask not what your country can do for you," he'd orated so handsomely during his first inauguration, "—but what you can do for your country."

But what did he do for his country during his second term?

I rush back to my room, the great-man theory of history turning sour in my mouth. But history couldn't be an experimental science until now.

During President Kennedy's first thousand days, he'd led us through two scary Cuban adventures, and we hadn't lost faith. He'd launched his Peace Corps and our first tiny space satellite. He had promised far-reaching foreign and domestic programs. He'd radiated confidence at a time when we still had faith in ourselves, and sometimes in our leaders.

I worry about my timing estimates back to November 22, 1963. I consider three possibilities, stemming from a few seconds' miscalculation in either direction, and from his reactions.

I stare at my disarranged bookshelves, searching for any speeches after the disturbing one he had planned to give at the Dallas Trade Mart. Instead there's a book I've never seen before, titled *The Shining Lance*. That sounds promising.

The beginning of the book describes a familiar scene: the motorcade passing through Dallas. This author at first quoted Manchester: "The Lincoln moved ahead at 11.2 miles an hour. It passed the tree. Zapruder, slowly swinging his camera to the right, found himself photographing the back of a freeway sign. Momentarily the entire car was obscured. But it was no longer hidden from the sixth-floor corner window."

Same as before, came the sudden sound of the first shot.

But the story then changed.

As the President's head had snapped forward and back when the driver gunned the engine, Jacqueline turned to him. The car continued its course, then there was a metallic clang as a second shot ricocheted from the rear bumper. A Secret Service agent ran, shouting. A third bullet slipped diagonally into the back of the driver's seat, miraculously missing everybody, but almost on target again.

The secret agent vaulted onto the back of the slowly moving convertible, crushing the president to shield him, although there was no fourth shot. The Lincoln lunged forward, gaining speed, rushing toward Parkland Memorial Hospital.

Hospital?

I read about how the president's terrible throat wound gurgled blood.

I can't endure reading these details.

I failed to disrupt the first shot. Apparently I should have set the timer several seconds further back into 1963. Or perhaps there were other reasons that bullet tore through JFK's neck.

At least I had disturbed the second shot since it struck the rear bumper this time. But the third shot was nearly on target again. It seemed that the tremendous wattage from my device, diminishing through thirty years like lightning, had amounted to such a small spark in Oswald's brain, it had only shaken him for a moment. My influence had only covered a few seconds.

Fortunately, Oswald hadn't attempted a fourth shot, and at least I had reached him. Any brain is a sensitive receiving instrument. But my primitive signaling device, probing the past with my clumsy electro-magnetic equivalent of a Neanderthal spear, had only caused Oswald to wince, and not soon enough. His first shot was still there. But did JFK suffer, because of me?

Scanning my shelves, I see tattered 1964 *LIFE* magazines I apparently collected this time around. I open several, searching for images of the President. I wonder if his neck wound left him incapacitated and frustrated, like Woodrow Wilson after his stroke, with Mrs. Wilson his intermediary—sometimes with her seeming in charge of the executive branch. I'm hoping Jackie didn't have to …

Then I read that after the President was wounded, a nurse of his claimed to have overheard conversations from behind his bed-screen. She heard the President attempt a laugh, gasping to his brother that there was at least one vote against him in Texas. He wanted to question the idiot.

JFK was then told Oswald was dead, shot even while being guarded by a multitude of law officers, silenced by a bar owner who might have mafia or other connections.

The president reportedly fell silent behind that screen.

My heart sinks as I continue to read.

The President heard that Oswald, a U.S. Marine, had strangely defected to the Soviet Union, later returning to the U.S. For what? To demand fair play for Cuba? The FBI hadn't notified the Secret Service of his background. It was unconscionable that Oswald had been employed in a building on the motorcade route and hadn't been under their surveillance.

JFK wheezed something about another chance for confrontation. It was not yet clear whether he was referring to Castro, Khrushchev, or someone else.

Rumors of his unfitness spread among Republicans. Although public sympathy raised his ratings, Congressmen saw him as weaker. Kennedy writhed on his bed, issuing angry orders.

I remember how, back in 1961, two years before his assassination attempt and when he was new to the office, he'd been trapped and humiliated by the Bay of Pigs debacle. He had become determined to push back harder. A year later, when the Soviets sneaked offensive missiles into Cuba, he'd made them blink. Khrushchev had withdrawn his missiles, and the Soviets gained JFK's promise not to invade Cuba. But Castro had survived... like a thorn in JFK's body.

I continue reading this new history.

Reportedly, Kennedy couldn't sleep so called for his brother Bobby, saying his wound would give him worldwide support and another chance at retribution against Castro. Bobby protested.

Yet the President sent amphibious tanks to pound downtown Havana. I have new memories now, memories of a revised history. As a teen in L.A., I now recall glancing nervously at the sky while Mother stocked up at our supermarket. When radio broadcasts blasted Castro with accusations, he retreated to the hills.

Speedily successful combat unified most Americans. The President's ratings skyrocketed. He pushed stalled domestic legislation through Congress. Pain from his wound drove him to ferocious activity, including numerous television appearances—as if he feared his life would run out.

My heart pounds as I read this. His opportunity for greatness.

In 1964, his vocal cords rasping menacingly, but sounding less nuclear than Goldwater, JFK won reelection victoriously. In 1965, two years after I saved him, he declared, "Let history record that America defends its friends. How will it look to the rest of the world if we fail to increase aid, and our friends in Saigon are massacred?"

They had applauded thunderously as he clutched the lectern, wincing, his face swollen, unable to turn his neck. His painful gestures seemed stiff as his critic Nixon's, according to reporters.

He sent Phantom Jets to aid South Vietnamese forces and American troops to guard more air bases, plus entire divisions to block the trails from North Vietnam. He said he wouldn't be pushed around. Congressmen second-guessed him, and he became increasingly irritable. During 1967, three years after I'd saved him, he nearly doubled ground troops.

At least this second-term Kennedy expanded medical and educational programs, winning both hearts and minds. But in 1968, the surprising Tet Offensive overran our Green

Beret camps and the templed city of Hue. Just as in the first history, Vietcong aided by the North Vietnamese executed thousands of civilians.

I am horrified. I put the magazine down to wipe my eyes.

Now I read how JFK had cried in outrage and pain, saying the Bay of Pigs should have taught him to never back down. Since that damned shooter destroyed his neck, it was only fair to finish off Castro in Cuba. He ordered B-52s to bomb Hanoi to rubble. Force that old Ho Chi Minh underground! But the North Vietnamese did not surrender, able to function and fight without a capital city.

With more than a million Americans bogged down in South Vietnam, Kennedy's second term was ending bitterly. Even his domestic programs were starving. High expectations burned like the jungles.

I was eighteen in 1968, when draft-age students demonstrated violently for peace. The thin paper of promises was ripped through by racial riots.

Even the president's brothers second-guessed him, JFK grimaced, saying "Robert, go run on the beach or run for the Senate or something. Let Lyndon run with my mistakes." But to everyone's surprise, Vice President Lyndon Johnson declined running in 1968, preferring peace and health on his little ranch beside the river.

I wonder: might Johnson have been better than this Kennedy who had survived with such bitterness, because of me?

JFK's physical condition reportedly deteriorated, due to chronic complications from his wound and adrenal insufficiency. His smile was swollen from years of cortisone injections. Then Bobby was murdered in a Los Angeles hotel, during his California primary victory rally. The lively senator Humphrey captured the Democratic nomination, promising tough peace with honor. Nixon, promising even tougher peace with honor, triumphantly moved into the White House.

I thought I'd changed history! But no, same year, same negativism in this new future—even after I saved JFK's life. I realize that my intervention had caused history to split into alternate, parallel tracks in the same country, same world but by 1969 the tracks nearly converged. As JFK lay in the hospital after another neck operation, Nixon prepared to subpoena him, to root out any last chance for an inspirational Kennedy legend.

Because of me, his life was extended, but in pain and humiliation. At times he said he wished he hadn't been born, even wished he'd never entered politics.

I won't accept this. I still believe if he hadn't been wounded and in constant pain, he would have become a great president.

I begin reassembling my equipment. I will try for a third and hopefully better version of JFK's history. I want to believe it was only his pain which made him act so aggressively. As if this is a play, I will rewrite it, with one blinding flash.

Second Try

Since I desperately believe it was my fault he failed, I know if I properly help, he will succeed. I can't risk being stopped. In this airfreight shipment, along with my globular device, timer, and headset, is a concealed revolver I was issued for on-campus protection. If anyone discovers what I'm attempting, they may realize an altered past might eliminate them. They would no doubt eliminate me.

Settled again in that high rig, preparing to place the device, I hear a voice below me. "You're blocking traffic."

A leathery face grins up at me from a Dallas police car's open
    cockpit. My hands sweat.
    "This is my job," I say, hoping the public utility company hasn't noticed that its huge rig is misplaced.
    "You don't look right." A small man, he stands below me. "Get down, sir." Anonymous traffic roars past. "Your Heavy Equip License?"
    I grope in the pockets of my stolen coveralls. "Must've left it in my other pants."
    "Whoever you are," he drawls, "walk over to my wagon and put your fingerprints on the tube."
    I know he'll try to search me, so after climbing down, I stumble against the rear fender, falling, intending to slide the revolver out of sight. But when I glance up from my knees he's lunging at me with both hands open. I yell for him to stop.
    A strange spark passes through my brain and rising hand. My finger contracts and the revolver explodes between us deafeningly. Vomiting blood, he struggles. Horrified, I hoist him onto the front seat of his car, push him beneath the steering column, out of sight. But I still saw his soundless, contorted face attempting to shout for help before it relaxed. I sob. This policeman's life can't be as important as the President's.
    My eardrums pound so loudly, I don't hear traffic. I drag an insulated cable from the rig and make my high-voltage connection. This device needs more electrical power this time to disrupt Oswald's shots.
    I twist the timer knob further to the right than last time. But I can't hear the clicking, although the headphones encase my ears. I'm afraid one of the alligator clips has slipped off the battery terminal.
    I glance upward to the rig's bulbous tip. The device glitters across from the window where Oswald had peered out. My MASERs must focus their simultaneous energy-

surges to its target with precise timing. During lower-wattage experiments with test equipment, I carefully left electrical meters in recording positions to be reread days and weeks later. Thankfully, some of that mysteriously missing energy now reappears to trigger my device.

Now I'm blinking, and my ears are freed from the pressure.

1993 Redux

W hen I regain consciousness in Dallas, I'm shocked at what I see. I am surrounded by rubble, and the depository is gone. Somehow I make my way back to the airport. Flying home on a decrepit antique Boeing 747, I clutch my forehead and close my eyes. What have I done now?

This new 1993 L.A. looks strangely unfamiliar. In a panic, I rush home to find out what happened, to make sense of this strange old-new city.

In my basement lab, now the pipes on the ceiling are red-brown with rust, dripping like slow rain beside unrecognizable equipment. In the new past and future I've created, I must have scrounged through junk bins or undergraduate labs to have found such primitive hardware.

I blink at a poster, drooping from my damp concrete wall. On it is a woman's face—pale, gaunt, gray-haired, and stern as a mother's. I don't recognize her and can't comprehend the printed command below her face.

I lurch to my bookshelves. There I see a massive book, another history, this time titled: *Victory*. Victory? That doesn't make sense. Clinging to the book, I look around. I unlock my iron door and limp a service tunnel, carrying the book upward. Daylight is rain-greyed, as if even the L.A. November weather was affected this time.

From the rain-gleaming quad, where no cars are parked, a long line of chatting people approach. They look like gray ants with flowery umbrellas. In the damp heat, surprisingly short-haired coeds in gray jumpsuits collapse umbrellas before entering the physics building.

I walk inside with them. Despite my presence, some unzip the fronts of their suits to air themselves, sighing and giggling instead of going to their learning booths. Some very pretty girls glance at me.

But my gaze is captured by a blazing red and orange abstract poster: NEVER AGAIN. Along the walls are hundreds of hand-painted posters. DOMINATE. IT'S NEVER TOO LATE.

They've messed up the Hall of Physics with sloppy posters.

IGNORANT, IGNORANT PROFESSORS. Staring at a poorly drawn, poster-cartoon of a familiar face, I feel my blood pressure rise. It's a blunt middle-age male face glaring back at me from the poster, a man whose cheek is darkly stained. My hand goes to my scarred face and suddenly I remember a blinding flash, like lightning, into my living room back when I was a teen. Burned.

These smooth-cheeked, bright-eyed, gleaming girls have all been born since then. I see another poster with that familiar hollow-cheeked, huge-eyed woman's face, grey hair spread as if on a pillow, with the caption: REMEMBER HER SACRIFICE. Who was she?

One girl stares at me. At my hip? I am only forty-three, but my body feels terribly old this time. She glares at the thick book I've carried into the building. She whispers to another girl, pointing at the book.

I turn my back. As if from habit, I hide the book's title against my body. Shrill voices rise as I retreat out of the building and back to the service tunnel, back to my hideaway. None follow me. The uneven thumping is my weak foot, weaker leg. I'm afraid to touch my face again.

I lurch into my basement room. No mirrors. I stare again at the gaunt-faced woman on the poster, feeling guilty for her hollow cheeks and dark staring eyes yet unsure if she was a politician or a saint.

I open that thick book called *Victory*, to search for Kennedy's name.

Same as before, in the first chapters I read how his convertible in that motorcade approached the Texas School Book Depository. My heart contracts with remembered agony. Why didn't they at least put on the convertible's bubble-top? Was it machismo for him to expose himself that way in a hostile city?

I read how his smile flashed, just before a sound like a firecracker exploded and a branch fell from a large oak tree. As his limousine moved further beyond the tree, another rifle-report overlapped a glassy smashing sound as the Lincoln's right rear stoplight shattered. The President had looked to the right at startled people lining the sidewalk. Puzzled, he had faced forward again as his driver stamped on the gas pedal, snapping JFK's luxuriant hair back with the acceleration. He may have opened his mouth to say something.

As a third shot sounded, the President had looked to his left, his expression contorted, his hand rising to his red-spattered left cheek. Seeing Jackie, he shrieked soundlessly and tried to cover her with his body. Amidst shouting, the driver raced the car hopelessly to Parkland Hospital.

During disorganized questioning, Oswald's sneering face shrunk as the President's yelling face confronted him. Oswald denied that he had retreated to his apartment to reappear with a concealed pistol. He denied having been halted by a police officer and murdering him. He denied fleeing into the movie theater, where he was finally arrested. But obviously his third, wild, rifle-shot had shattered Jacqueline's skull.

I am reading this new history, thoroughly overcome. Oh, Jackie. What have I done now?

Yet I persist. I read how the next afternoon, when the President had lifted his swollen face from his pillow, his voice thick from sedatives, he had glared at his brother. "Does Castro have brainwashing stuff to do that to a man?"

Bobby muttered that a psychopath acting alone was probably a better explanation.

"Alone?" JFK blurted, "Why is that the best explanation? So we can keep turning the other cheek?"

Bobby had hung his head and squeezed his knuckles.

"Psychopath acting alone?" the President cried out. "No, a puppet, used psychopaths, preparing men like missiles. It had to be Castro. What he did to my wife shows me his threat. With the intercontinental missiles he's still building he'll first-strike us."

He cried out to heaven while Bobby's restraining hands clung to his shoulders, arguing that they must wait for an investigation.

"Investigate till doomsday," the President had retorted, according to this *Victory* author unknown to me. "You're my Attorney General. Select a commission. Hide from reality if you think we need a long report."

With Bobby decoyed from the center of power, the President gathered other advisers, the same men he'd assembled a year previous, in 1962, during the Cuban Missile Crisis. Instead of relying on normal diplomatic channels through the State Department, he prepared to use military force without openly consulting Congress, so great was his distress at losing Jackie.

Considering a naval quarantine of Cuba, some advisers suggested surgical airstrikes followed by amphibious landings—possibly killing a few Russian technicians. It would more massively clean up Cuba, calling Khrushchev's bluff while we could still get away with it.

In this revised November 1963, the *Victory* narrative indicated that the so-called missile gap was decisively in our favor. Most Soviet missiles were of intermediate range, merely capable of devastating Western Europe. According to the CIA, Khrushchev's few operational intercontinental missiles were unreliable. Easy targets.

"We have another chance," the newly-saved President had reportedly said with eerie calm, "to police Cuba. Meanwhile, we'll begin a Strategic Air Command exercise. You saw what happened to my wife," he continued, as if there were a logical connection.

His advisers were silent.

"Confrontation is the only way to meaningfully deal with that maniac," the President said. "But, if you're still worried, I can get on the hotline and personally inform him our bombers are a public relations feint, for domestic political reasons."

Some exchanged disturbed glances.

"Khrushchev shouldn't panic," the President added. "His agents will report we are staying above ground. None of us will be helicoptering to shelters. We're offering a safe way out for him."

As Tank Landing Ships turned toward Cuba, worldwide radio stations denounced Castro. After an airstrike killed him, supposedly U.S. troops had seized conclusive evidence that Castro had ordered the assassination of our president and his wife.

Khrushchev, instead of immediately disassociating himself from Fidel, angrily issued ultimatums. If the United States broke that 1962 agreement and occupied Cuba, there would be terrible consequences. He would fly to the UN.

Americans laughed with relief.

As Khrushchev's plane glinted high over Greenland, he was allowed to see B-52 bombers flashing in the other direction. His jet transmitted in code to the Soviet Union. As he descended into morning thunder clouds along our North American coast and landed at the far end of New York's Idlewood Airport, he was surrounded by police cars. Khrushchev just waved and smiled at the distant TV cameras and ducked into a black limousine. It was not a convertible.

From the Soviet Union Premier's expected route to Manhattan Island, police herded placard-bearing protesters crazed by continuous jackhammer news coverage. But most New Yorkers went about their business, cursing the morning rain. I, still a wheezing adolescent in L.A., sat watching television, home due to smog.

While Khruschev's motorcade followed a devious route, his rain-lashed limousine creeping toward the glassy, slab-sided UN building, lightning flickered through the clouds. Signals bounced back and forth between Washington and our missile installations. From the dry planes of North Dakota, a single primitive 1963 liquid-fuel missile nosed like a cautious prairie dog from its underground silo.

It suddenly pointed, as if its system's brain-like maze had received official coding. Or perhaps both firing officers misread a lightning-distorted signal. Or perhaps months before, when this missile was assembled, a secret bypass receiver had been inserted by someone—or some group— with a remote radio-trigger. Perhaps even its complex circuitry had been madly time-probed by someone in some more desperate future.

Regardless, the missile lurched upward with a roar, springing at the heavens like an uncontrollable beast from mankind's past. That lone missile irretrievably gained speed, moving faster than an assassin's bullet. Amazement, panic, and chagrin were expressed by many in our military communications network. While New Yorkers thought about lunch, the President decided our best remaining option was to launch remaining missiles. There was static on the Hotline and a recorded message.

As Khrushchev's limousine crawled like a wet black bug toward the shimmering, tombstone-shaped UN building, Manhattan Island was brightly air-blasted by an enormous Soviet ICBM, successfully launched during their instinctive counterstrike. When ours went up, so had theirs.

It's strange for me to have new memories now. I now recall boyhood amazement at the L.A. sky brightening through the window without warning. Although filtered by protective layers of smog, the airburst blinded me to shadows. Many seconds later, a thunderclap blasted the window glass inward. I had rolled in glass, screamed for help, smelled smoke.

That big, dirty missile had exploded nearer San Diego. Lucky for us, that was downwind from the cloud. I remember something else, which seemed trivial at that time: Dallas was also air-blasted that day.

As I see this terrible revised history in *Victory*, this has terrible implications for me, for my part in all of it.

I read more. Flying past mushroom clouds from our first-strike missiles, flocks of our SAC bombers methodically made Soviet cities and concentration camps equally radioactive. Winning, the United States suffered less than 30 million immediate casualties. Without Moscow, the USSR seemed to come apart.

With inspiring leadership from Lyndon Johnson— providentially far from Washington on that explosive day, barbecuing steaks at his ranch, surviving Americans used bulldozers to bury faceless fellow citizens. Soon afterward,

Johnson took his presidential oath of office at a temporary capital beside the Pedernales River. His reassuring speeches were as full of macho as Texas chili. He announced this would never happen again. Because we had become the major nuclear power, it was our duty to prevent more threats to world peace.

Johnson's best and brightest advisers suggested turning the focus to Vietnam. Send more draftees clutching rifles.

I'm sweating. All versions of our history converged in Vietnam, yet for some reason I always end up in this concrete room. Apparently not only my asthma, but also boyhood injuries from that Soviet blast south of L.A., kept me out of the Vietnam draft to still be admitted to grad school here.

No matter how I alter history, young men are always dispatched to peace-threatening jungles and deserts. Left were women in majority, who elected a woman president, only to lose her to Victory carcinoma. That must be her, eyes staring from a frame of gray hair upon a hospital pillow, with the caption: REMEMBER HER SACRIFICE. Other women suffering from Victory fallout stagger through the Memorial Ruins of Washington to its hallowed ground zero. Crying and cursing, they hurl glassy rubble at the tall bronze Memorial Victory Statue of John F. Kennedy.

I can't believe he triggered the first aberrant missile. But he was led toward confrontation, like Oswald, shaped by a cultural heritage of legendary folk heroes, quick-draw cowboys, stern-jawed military men, and boyhood American macho dreams. Because his wife was murdered before millions of viewers, he had to do something bold.

Now thirty years later, my cheek is still stiff from that ancient flash burn and I limp from slowly spreading prostate cancer. We are permeated by the past.

Less than an hour ago, if my hand had twisted the timer knob so far to the right, Oswald's wild third shot would have missed Jacqueline's skull. Millions of lives might have been saved.

I know Dallas hasn't been rebuilt and lacks electrical power. If this were a play, the stage for beginning its third act in parallel was destroyed thirty years ago.

But JFK was a man who projected hope, so I will try again.

Third Try

This aged plane drags its shadow across the ruins of Dallas and lands beyond Fort Worth, which had been upwind at the time of the air blast. After the war, downtown Dallas was declared a perpetual memorial to Texas heroes. Its ground zero is now surrounded by metro mess.

My rental sedan passes bent Dallas road signs. I blink at eyeless buildings landscaped by sagebrush. I drive along crumbling Houston Street more slowly than JFK's motorcade, approaching the left turn onto Elm Street.

This immense mound of heat-fused rubble must have been the Texas School Book Depository. There is nothing but sky now where that sixth-floor window once was. I measure from the curb, trying to locate where I stood last time beside a rig no longer here.

Over piles of shattered brickwork, a crow caws, circling. A scrubby young oak has risen from the rubble. As I pick up loose bricks, something moves at the edge of my vision. Odd. I feel as if I'm observing myself. A ragged bum watches me build a pillar of bricks where I previously stood beside the rig those other times. I stack bricks as high as my shoulders, creating a headless brick-man, smiling wryly.

While the wind swirls dust, I open the trunk of the rental sedan and carefully I lift out the heavy globular device now reconstructed from strange old parts. I place it on the pillar, where its glittering shell reflects the distorted ruins of Dallas and my own face with ancient flash burns. I don't want this all to end where JFK is remembered only as a man who led us into the valley of the shadow of death.

I breathe the city's dust. There's not enough electrical power here for another implosion to reach back thirty years, or even thirty days. I seem trapped in this new creation. It may seem that there's no direct way now for me to probe back to Oswald's head, six stories above me in its own time.

But what man can imagine, man will attempt—my own version of an old Jules Verne quote. I still believe in JFK as a man with intelligence, who with enough courage and energy and without extreme grief could positively shape the future. But no matter what, this current new history I'm in is unacceptable.

So as before, I connect my timer box to the low-voltage side of the device. But this time the circuits are short. I have no need to extend my MASER device six stories up a rig. I set my globular device instead on my brick pillar, for I have a new plan.

I limp around to its high-voltage side. Only a few hours in my time, traffic had roared on that other contemporary Elm Street when I had connected my thick high-voltage cable to the tremendous electrical power of Dallas to probe back thirty years. Now I simply hope to reach back a few hours to the last Dallas when I last stood beside the rig.

This globe's shiny surface reflects my scarred smile. Under the sedan's raised hood, I clamp to one high-voltage terminal a thin red jumper wire, to the other, a black wire. In my earlier test experiments, twelve volts didn't implode far into the past. I check the chronometers. I hope my device overlaps one or both of my heads where I stood beside the rigs in the other realities.

I don my headset. The timer-box clicks loudly in my ears in this desolately quiet street. I check my stopwatch.

Thirty years ago, the motorcade was approaching. The police motorcycles of JFKs escort advancing along Houston Street, toward the Texas School Book Depository.

I look at my brick-man's glittering head. I glance at my parked rental sedan: HERTZ LIVES. The motorcycles would now be—have been—turning left onto Elm.

Now I click twelve volts into this gleaming globe at the same moment my hands in the other realities are—were—still twisting their timer knobs. I am hoping the shocks will twitch their—my hands further to the right before their timers release the tremendous electrical power of Dallas to the devices atop the rigs.

With two chances, I hope at least one of those devices implodes sooner.

Most likely Oswald's finger was already on the trigger of his rifle as the motorcycles turned below him onto Elm Street. Following the lead car, an unmarked sedan was driven by the police chief. On Houston Street, the President's gleaming convertible approached Oswald as he must have been deciding when to shoot.

The other times he waited and as the limousine began its left turn, he would have needed to shift his body.

The clicking stops.

The Fourth Reality

This time I saw no blinding flash. The tiny implosion within the device wouldn't leave enough heat to burst it. But my globular device has vanished. And there, marvel of marvels, stands the Texas School Book Depository, rising in the sky over immaculate streets bustling once again with traffic. I rush eagerly to the Dallas airport, eager to see what new reality I've created.

As my plane—now startlingly ultra-modern—descends to Los Angeles International Airport, I see huge gaps in the basin's mountain ranges. Canyons have been gouged out as if by mechanical glaciers, evidently to improve air circulation. As the plane turns, looking toward the Pacific, I discover where all that dirt and rock was moved. Curving out beyond Santa Monica, a widespread peninsula glitters with connected ponds. Steam rises from mounds topped by saucers.

Apparently they're using the power transmissions from sunlight satellites to produce freshwater and marine minerals. They must also be splitting distilled water into oxygen and hydrogen, then using hydrogen to fortify hydrocarbons. I observe LNG tankers entering the outer harbor floating high in the water, while those leaving are deeply loaded. We must be exporting liquefied natural gas. Do we finally have a trade surplus?

On the horizon, the profile of Catalina Island looks altered, a neat island cone beyond it as if raised by a controlled man-made volcano. Satellites are visible in the daylight. They are thinking BIG this time.

Walking briskly across the quad, under an incredibly blue LA sky, I inhale the moist freshness of newly mown lawns. No sneezing! Apparently they've tackled more than the water shortage. Students appear neatly dressed. Youthful faces look preoccupied. I'm the only person peering up in wonder at an immense saucer supported on pylons above the freeway. Shaped like a tremendous microwave receiver, it's aimed upward.

As if from habit, I press my thumbprint on the LA Times dispenser. A fotostrip emerges with gray details. A senator complains because overall inflation has reached 2%, and there is disgraceful 3% unemployment because of armament reductions. The daily fee for recharging a car is expected to go up at least 5% next year, due to cost overruns for the High Sunlight Series of orbiting electrical focuses. Another committee has been formed to protest the six-month work year.

I'm wondering ... what do they *want?*

My news strip flutters in a dry land-breeze as I hold it tight. Believe it or not, I read that the current President's popularity is declining. The opposition says he lacks inventiveness.

I am amazed by the dissatisfaction.

Back in my basement room, I notice the pipes on the ceiling have been caulked, and on the concrete walls a new 1993 calendar displays a smiling young lady's charms instead of that depressing former poster. My work counter is bountifully stacked with expensive equipment. Apparently I've received a larger grant but made less progress toward some goal. I blink at shelves of history books.

But for some reason, I'm still assembling a device here. My palms sweat.

When I glance at the books I've collected this time, I am now confronted by: *The Great Failure of John F. Kennedy.* Surprised and outraged by this title, I curse the author. Yet I'm afraid he knows things I don't remember yet. My hands tremble as I turn pages.

In the first chapter, the president's motorcade moved along Houston Street on the same route to the Dallas Trade Mart for his speech. But before turning left onto Elm Street, there was a loud report, as if a motorcycle backfired. His limousine had continued majestically toward the Texas School Book Depository and made the turn but slowed down. Newsmen noticed steamy water spraying the pavement beneath the Lincoln's hood.

An agent ran alongside, shouting. He vaulted onto the rear of the convertible as it passed beneath the oak tree and tried to hurl himself on top of the president. But JFK squirmed aside, as if not wanting the heavily zealous agent to crush him and aggravate his old back injury. Then he had shoved the man across Jackie.

They struggled in the back seat while the car gained speed beyond the tree. It pulled out to the left and at high-speed led the motorcade passing the police lead car and the motorcyclist. All pursued the President's limousine for several miles until it suddenly turned right on an exit ramp and stopped.

The President stood up in the convertible, beckoning the police lead sedan alongside. The agent pulled him down again. Agents, advisers, and politicians ran from other halted cars. They feared the unknown gunman might have followed as well. As they crowded around the President's limousine with hood raised, arguments erupted. One advisor wanted them all to squeeze into the agent's follow-up convertible. Another suggested that they should displace the Vice-President from his own automobile at the end of the line.

Before anyone could stop him, the President scrambled out of his stalled convertible. He peered over the shoulders of all the amateur mechanical experts, and wrinkled his nose at the hot smell from the engine. As no more water squirted from its radiator, he finally turned and grinned at Jacqueline, huddled safely in the back seat.

I can't understand why there had only been one shot.

Reading further, I see that disregarding his advisers and other devoted men trying to be human shields, JFK had walked around to Jacqueline's door to open it with a sweeping gesture. She smiled at this gallantry and descended to the pavement like a princess. They squeezed into the unmarked lead sedan with an agent plus the governor and his wife, compressing the police chief, still at the wheel. The sedan then led the motorcade along a different route toward the Dallas Trade Mart.

Reportedly the President said something about convertibles. It was not complementary.

The chief turned up the volume of excited voices on the sedan's two-way radio. Secret Service agents who had stayed with the stranded convertible were reporting the bullet must have been fired from a high angle, the way it penetrated the front of the radiator. It had probably come from an upper floor of that book warehouse.

Several lawmen had already entered the Texas School Book Depository. Others questioned witnesses who had frantically pointed at an upper corner window after the motorcade passed by.

On the sixth floor, no gun or expended shell was found. Yet an odd arrangement of boxes beside the window was noted. From that spot, a policeman looking out the window had direct sight along Houston Street. Shifting his body, turning his head to the right, the officer had a good view along Elm Street, except where obscured by the oak tree.

In front of the building, depository workers accounted for each other to the police. One said he had noticed Oswald looking angry as he left, as if he'd been in a fistfight. He looked as if his eye had been punched by someone wearing a ring.

As for which way Oswald had walked, or whether he had hailed a cab, there was confusion. Many agreed he had been carrying a long package.

Police interviewed others about the grassy knoll, from which some said they thought they heard a second shot. Also suspicious movements had been reported near the overpass. This and other information was radioed to the Secret Service agents at the Trade Mart, where the President shrugged and grinned nervously. "I'm going to go ahead— if they can't shoot any better than that."

In the Trade Mart auditorium, loud applause punctuated the beginning of the President's speech. At least he began his speech as pre-released to the press that morning. *Most* Texans assembled in the Trade Mart applauded. Outside, more than two hundred lawmen looked anxious. They hustled away three men with placards and spoke into portable radios. Inside, nervous Secret Service agents scanned the audience, unsure what to look for … a white male with a black eye?

As JFK continued his speech, he took a deep breath as faces in the audience uplifted to his. He smiled as if he weren't a constant target.

But as I read this new history, I'm wondering, what had happened to Oswald? Where was he?

I considered his black eye. Through the scope sight, Oswald must have studied his target in the distance. Yet as it approached, he hesitated for some reason. Each other time, he'd waited until the limousine turned onto Elm Street, carrying the President away from him.

But this time my shocks came sooner. Thirty years after that fateful moment, in the ruins of Dallas, I triggered my device on a head-high pillar of bricks. Its tiny implosion, probing back a few hours into contemporary Dallas, must have overlapped one of my heads.

When my wrist twitched further to the right, the timer set back in time. As the President's convertible headed toward the building, my device at the tip of the rig must have imploded sooner—just as Oswald shifted his position, rifle scope dipping.

I suspect that the shock to his brain made his finger contract, causing his rifle to blast and recoil its hard-edged scope against his eye-socket. Perhaps he cursed or whimpered. Momentarily blinded, he probably worked his rifle-bolt. Blinking his eyes, he would have twisted to the right, just as the watery car blurred into that fuzzy tree, then accelerated away from the motorcade.

How I wish I'd seen Oswald's battered face as he clutched his rifle-stock, white knuckled. Hurriedly he must have disassembled his rifle, rewrapped it, and pocketed the fired cartridge. This time he had reason to take his rifle with him disguised in a box for curtain rods.

Less smoothly than the other times he'd left the building, he walked through the commotion on the ground floor and disappeared. Later, police tried to find out if he had caught a cab nearby, and where it might have gone. Officers patrolled the streets.

Meanwhile, in the Trade Mart, nearing the end of his speech, the president's voice rose: "… a nation can be no stronger abroad than she is at home. Only an America which practices what it preaches about equal rights and social justice will be respected by those whose choice affects our future. Only an America which has fully educated its citizens is fully capable of tackling complex problems and perceiving the hidden dangers of the world in which we live. And only an America which is growing and prospering economically can sustain the worldwide defenses of freedom, while demonstrating to all concerned the opportunities of our system and our society."[1]

As the President continued his speech, their masked faces were silent.

"We in this country, in this generation, are—by destiny rather than choice—the watchmen on the walls of world freedom. We ask, therefore, that we may be worthy of our power and responsibility, that we may exercise our strength with wisdom and restraint, and that we may achieve in our time and for all time the ancient vision of 'peace on Earth, goodwill toward men.' That must always be our goal, and the righteousness of our cause must always underlie our

---

1. This quote and the one following are verbatim from Remarks Prepared for Delivery at the Trade Mart in Dallas, TX, November 22, 1963 [Undelivered], housed at the John F. Kennedy Presidential Library and Museum. https://www.jfklibrary.org/archives/other-resources/john-f-kennedy-speeches/dallas-tx-trade-mart-undelivered-19631122

strength. For as was written long ago, 'Except the Lord keep the city, the watchman waketh but in vain.'"[2]

But as he began to depart from his original speech, there was uneven applause. Many of the Texans assembled felt they had been preached at unnecessarily. Afterward he joked about his poor reception, but said he was more interested in the future of the nation.

While JFK flew back to Washington, the FBI discovered that Oswald failed to appear with any package at his apartment to hang curtain rods. He seemed to have vanished from the face of the earth, defaulting on child support payments. He left the Texas School Book Depository short one worker—although was easily replaced from the ranks of the unemployed.

Then the investigation abruptly submerged.

The President Kennedy I'd saved sent more Green Berets to assist the South Vietnamese. He avoided discussing the Oswald affair. During his 1964 reelection campaign, he talked nearly as tough as Goldwater, but certain politicians whispered he could not live through a second term due to his having Addison's Disease. He was expected to weaken and eventually lapse into a coma. His face was swollen from continual cortisone injections.

However, his family insisted it was merely an adrenal insufficiency—that occasional injections kept him healthy as a horse. Apparently, while serving his country in the South Pacific during World War II, malaria could have affected his adrenal glands. Yet he fully expected to outlive most of his critics, grinning while saying, "I'm younger."

During his first four years in office he felt restrained by the narrowness of his victory. He cautiously held back from pushing many campaign promises through a Congress

2. In real life, Kennedy's assassination prevented delivery of them, but the undelivered speech was available for citizens to read.

dominated by senior chairmen who considered him an upstart.

But at the beginning of his second term—I'd like to say thanks to me—after a decisive 1964 victory over Goldwater, he influenced more Congressmen. His civil rights, medical, housing, and education bills passed and his New Frontier Program gained momentum.

Unfortunately, the Vietnam War continued. Increasing draft calls reduced his popularity on campuses to zero. Congress voted for enormous sums for the military, at the expense of JFK's domestic programs. Thousands of Americans came home in body bags.

JFK became determined to end involvement in Vietnam. When heated discussions led to the same unacceptable alternatives, he stated that a president is always trapped into trying to look like a winner to voters and historians.

"When my term ends this year, I'll be too young to retire gracefully from public life. I may run as a senator, to hang onto as much power in the party as possible. That might help Robert rise. Help Ted. But I have other considerations." He smiled sadly. "All profile, no courage?" This President—who I had saved—said he was in a better position to get us out of Vietnam than the next one who would have to come in looking strong and staying popular. "So what if I go down in history as the President who lost the war?"

His advisors shouted, horrified. They warned he'd be deserting loyal Vietnamese to certain death and humiliate our powerful military forces. They declared that he'd show our allies they couldn't trust our leader to stand by them. He'd embarrass American voters. He'd break up the Democratic Party and let his family down. He would lose his place in history.

Still, he persisted in considering a withdrawal.

They wanted him to keep his plans secret, at least until after the voting in November.

In his chair he rocked back and forth, faster.

"Do any of you think, as a lame duck president in December, in my last month I'll have the influence to start pulling us out of Vietnam?"

Some of his political advisers nodded frantically.

"I must start sooner than that, if it's to be done gracefully," he said. "Don't want it to turn into a bug-out."

But someone promptly leaked his withdrawal plan. The panicky Saigon regime collapsed in September. JFK announced that sending more U.S. troops would be counterproductive, so began pulling them out while the unprepared Communists closed in on Saigon.

The final bug-out left billions of dollars' worth of trucks, tanks, planes, and supplies—not as much as the other times, but five years sooner. Some lives were saved, at least.

When Kennedy ran for a third term in 1968, most Americans still believed we could have won, should have won in Vietnam. One well-known politician was quoted as saying, "He will be a stain forever on our American flag." Accepting blame as he had for the Bay of Pigs debacle, JFK tried to be the lone scapegoat. But now all Kennedys were being criticized and the Democratic Party accused of giving away Vietnam. Consequently, in November 1968, a smiling Richard Nixon was overwhelmingly elected President of the United States.

President Nixon underspent funds Congress had allocated for JFK's New Frontier Programs. He spoke enthusiastically of our return to a free-market, free-enterprise system, yet mysteriously, the economy staggered with both a recession and inflation. Nixon attacked media troublemakers. He seemed baffled and indecisive, blaming economic problems on the increased cost of oil, on the environmentalists, and on Democrats for the loss of Vietnam.

He was easily reelected, as there was no Watergate exposure in 1973, yet financial indiscretions led to the Vice-President being replaced by Gerald Ford. By then, stagflation was uncontrollable. The country drifted. Little was being done to reach national energy goals the President had expressed earlier.

On my bottom shelf, in a folder of yellowed newspaper clippings, I see how our history nearly converged in 1976. Vice-President Ford ran for President when there was 8% unemployment and 10% inflation. Most people simply voted their pocketbooks. A dark horse Democrat, Carter, narrowly won that election. President followed president while Congress squabbled. National unity inspired by World War II dissipated. American voters lost direction.

Long before this, the wry book *The Great Failure of John F. Kennedy* was published. In that, blame for current problems could be assigned to the past.

That is, until 1980.

New Inspiration

"Have we produced a generation of blobs?" The handsome white-haired guest on at late-night TV talk show leaned toward an invisible audience. "I refuse to believe it. 1980s young people are our most essential resource. They have energy. Free their creativity, and they will produce wonders beyond our dreams.

"Listen to the doers, to the purposeful. Don't express opposition without alternatives, find fault without favor, perceive gloom on every side nor seek influence without responsibility. I said something like that years ago, in a speech in Dallas. It's still true today."

He reminded nodding late-night viewers of our energetic history, of those who "rode the first waves of the industrial revolution, the first waves of modern invention, and the first wave of nuclear power," referring to another speech he'd given in Houston, in '62. "We did not intend to founder in the coming age of space."

Appearances on small college campuses grew to larger venues. He emerged from retirement to find increasing interest in his words, talking his way across the country.

I especially love one quote from him I found in a torn clipping: "Our future can be shaped like a symphony." My heart pounds. I'm anxious to see this old man. I imagine him cheering for his lively grandchildren as they play touch football on the lawn at Hyannis Port. I estimate that now, in 1993, he should be seventy-six years old.

In my concrete room, I stare at a device I'm still assembling for some reason. I have a strange thought. Might someone ahead of me in time, with more sophisticated equipment, be touching my brains, my world? I shudder. It is one thing to manipulate, another to be manipulated.

As I read a few more clippings from 1983, I suddenly feel crushed. During his 'radical pep-talk' to students at USC, he reportedly had trouble breathing. His bronchial infection didn't yield to antibiotics. Years on cortisone may have weakened his resistance. He gasped yet smiled from his oxygen tent at Jacqueline. The doctors were encouraging.

I tear up. She stuck by him all these years. She reportedly waved at him and he had said something—pointing upward.

During the night, an orderly entered. At least he wore a hospital orderly's uniform. When he removed his white mask, it was apparent that his bitter smile had become wrinkled with age. His revolver was rust-stained, as if it had been buried. Now he didn't miss.

In my concrete tomb—I mean, room—my fist crushes these tattered news clippings. 1983. My chest heaves. I've missed him by ten years.

I feel immense loneliness and doubt.

I blink at my MASER device. I want to believe with JFK we can manage our science, now as much part of our environment as wheatfields of earlier men. I stare at these neon metallic tools on my work counter. Breathing hard I reach for them.

From the summits of convex satellites, giant MASERs continuously aim at Earth, pulsing microwave power to skyward-facing reflective blue saucers across our land. Like blue flowers, they capture energy to enhance our lives. Is this a result of his years of leadership and influence?

I feel the joy of realization. So much we've accomplished since then, it seems that something greater than John F. Kennedy lives in us. We are a mosaic of millions of people. Not all remember him. Yet we inherited far more than an image whose fine voice once challenged us: "Ask not what your country can do for you, but what you can do for your country."

I must decide now.

I raise my ballpeen hammer. My arm muscles twitch, as if receiving conflicting signals from pasts or futures. I both sob and laugh. His time-tool was his life. This is mine.

With a resounding clang, I break open this incomplete device containing MASER crystals. My hammer strikes again and again. Glittering wreckage tinkles on the concrete floor. Finally, the only sound is my breathing.

I'm staying where he may have lived longest.

Where his legend lives.

THE MARCH OF TIME

A short story written in Santa Barbara, CA in the 1960s
Setting: A college campus somewhere on Earth

Because he thought we were voteless children, the Governor punished all for what a few had done. In helpless anger, although we had marched through the snow to the State Capital, the Governor said: "Welcome to the real world. I worked my way through college." Smiling, he listened to our childish abuse. As he departed, he strode past our bodies, limp in protest, on the marble steps. To him, our lie-in simply showed our political powerlessness.

"I stand up for what I believe in," the Governor said, as he sat on the soft leather seat in his limousine. As it purred away, some barefoot freak who haunts every college crowd shouted, "Legalize pot!" And the TV crew interviewed him, because the rest of us wore shoes and he was naturally more interesting.

We sang freedom songs. Mob psychologists insisted that singing was a displacement activity, like bulls pawing the earth instead of charging. George Gross had shouted for us to invade the State House, but we were singing with such loud pseudo-triumph no one could hear him. I could see George's fat face straining as if his sound had been turned off, his thick glasses glinting with despair. Even I knew we had passed our emotional climax.

By suppertime we had shot our wad. Hungry and tired of protesting, with sore feet like battle wounds, we felt we'd earned our bus ride. Homeward-bound, we hummed defiant songs as if returning from a football game. With girls' heads on our shoulders, we knew we had demonstrated our political power to the world. A moral victory! Except that I wasn't sitting next to a girl on the bus. I was stuck next to George Gross.

Some square chick shouted: "Wait till next year, Gov-er-nor," as if the rumbling bus were a football stadium. Everyone swayed and hummed or sang "'til next year..."

George Gross stood and shouted shrilly. "He doesn't come up for election for 3.5 more years. By that time, all of us who care will have graduated. We'll all be over twenty-one then, old enough to vote, but he won't be worried!

"In 3.5 years, we'll have pregnant wives and mortgage payments and be bitching about state taxes. In 3.5 years, if the Governor promises another tax cut, we'll think he's a sound economist. In 3.5 years, when tuition is goosed higher, it will seem unfortunate yet perhaps economically necessary. Painless, so we won't be here next time to protest. We won't be students anymore. We'll be taxpayers. That crud knows we'll change."

Personally, I would have been glad to forget the failure of our march. I would concentrate on better grades.

But George continued ranting. "Remember this Day of Infamy! In 3.5 years, when the Governor tries to get reelected, we've got to remember to vote as a bloc against him. Then vote analysis will show politicians that future students should be taken seriously."

He was still griping the next day while we fed chickens in our psych seminar. My term project was memory-imprinting in newly hatched chicks—a standard textbook project. Newborn chicks, shown their first large moving object at birth, should follow that—me—forever. Like mom!

The chick's first recognition of me as "mother" was supposed to make a permanent impression in a temporary receptive area of its brain. To get an A on my lab project,

I'd need to report that my chicks, on seeing me shortly after being hatched, would avidly follow me. Indeed, my chicks scrambled after me with pitiful peeping. I felt huge and politically potent. Perhaps I could even be Student Body President, if the chicks who wore bras would vote for me.

George squawked at me from the next room to come hold his hen.

His project was to fix last year's chicken failures. Those few suspicious chicks who had refused to follow their pseudo-mothers were now mature, noisy hens, squawking hatred of humanity. A bit like George.

For his project, George was trying to re-open these hens' minds with a more powerful trip than LSD. "Grab her!" To make one hen more receptive to his revised imprint, George intended to momentarily blank her out. "Put on your helmet. Hold her tighter." He pressed the button of his psychoshocker. Its thirty-watt lightbulb glowed, then winked out.

Instantly recovering consciousness, the hen glimpsed George's plump hand offering her a plump mealworm. As her beak snapped up the mealworm, he hoped the hen's newly opened brain would imprint to love George for himself. Avidly, she pecked his plump finger. "Down, girl! That's enough. Grab her. Stick her back in her cage. Help me carry the other cages to the gym."

Later that night in the hollow basketball gym, George clunked down the heavy psychoshocker on the center jump. He plugged in the extension cord. We arranged the cages outward in concentric circles. The most distant hens squawked from the bleachers and from underneath the scoreboard.

Eyeing the psychoshocker, we put on our steel helmets. George twisted the rheostat all the way up, now lighting a hundred-fifty-watt bulb. When it blinked out, he rushed among the cages distributing mealworms.

"Now let them out," he said excitedly.

The sight of so many hens hungrily following George imprinted me with foul suspicions concerning human motivations. I decided right then that I'd transfer my major to Pre-Law.

While sitting in my last lecture, I blanked out. Then raising my head, along with my other classmates, I heard George's shrilly shouting voice. Through the loudspeakers, into every classroom, he shouted about student freedom.

"...Day of Infamy must be remembered. In 3.5 years, you *must* remember. Defeat the Governor!"

There was a clunk. Campus police must have dragged him away from the master-mic. My head hurt. I suspected George had blanked out everyone on campus with a high-wattage psychoshock during that last instant before we heard his voice. He had tried to imprint us.

But my headache faded. I felt unchanged, even though his electric power source had been the linear accelerator in the Physics Building, melting his psychoshocker. We all trooped outside to watch the firemen spraying the Physics Building. I never liked physics anyway.

The college administrators were displeased with George. The college had been investigated so much lately by the state legislature that our administrators tried to hush this up. They blamed the fire on a short circuit. They explained away our momentary unconsciousness, "due to an unusually warm Friday afternoon in the classrooms."

A few birds and people did follow each other around, but by the time I was admitted to law school, I had junked the incident in the ash heap of my subconscious. George was readmitted to the college, dieted off twenty pounds, and changed his major to Rocket Propulsion. I supposed his attempt at psychoshocking us politically had failed.

Although occasionally I'd wake up shouting "Day Of Infamy. Vote for revenge."

Two years later, from law school, I read that George was under investigation by the FAA, NASA, and perhaps the FBI for launching an unauthorized grapefruit-sized satellite. Even satellites that small were unauthorized because hobbyists were cluttering up the 24,901 orbit around Earth.

From the County Jail, George phoned me. He asked when I expected to graduate from law school—seeming to hope I'd defend him for free. He admitted that his grapefruit was on a station above the US but wouldn't tell me what it contained. I refused to give him free legal advice.

After serving ninety days, George lost another twenty pounds. He wasn't recognizable except for his thick glasses. He looked as cool as a junior executive with etchings and was readmitted again to the college as an Economics major. Changing his college major three times may have indicated he was not a stable person.

Occasionally he telephoned me in the middle of the night to shout: "Countdown. 3.5, 2.5, 1.5 years until we vote." I got an unlisted number as soon as Clairol and I returned home from our honeymoon and was careful not to invite him to our track-house.

By the end of 3.5 years, I had become Junior Partner in a law firm at the State Capital. What little money I earned was eroded by my wife's pregnancy expenses, and taxes on the house which our friendly neighborhood mortgage company owned. State and Federal income taxes devoured the rest. Too poor to eat lunch, I carried crackers in my briefcase. I was not pleased when I received a mimeographed form letter from George, pleading for me to remember the Day of Infamy, to remember student freedom, eradicate tuition, beat the Governor, VOTE!

Because it was near reelection day and George had sunk to mimeographed propaganda sheets, I assumed his grapefruit-sized memory fuse in the sky was a dud. I had thought it must contain a 3.5-year timer, set to trigger action in all who George had attempted to imprint years before, back when he'd psychoshocked us over the classrooms' loudspeaker.

Of course I didn't approve of all economic moves the Governor had made since then. I would have voted on the way home from the office. But I had to work late that Tuesday and the Governor would have been reelected anyway.

With the Governor's renewed mandate from the people, he made new appointments to the College Governing Board. He surprised those of us who hadn't paid much attention. To assist free enterprise, and reduce overpaid but immovably tenured faculty members, one board member announced:

"Hereafter, students in the upper 5% of their high school graduating classes will *not* be admitted to this public college. Tax-supported colleges should not compete with private universities for 'the cream of the crop.' In our American system, public institutions should compete as little as possible with private enterprise.

"In support of this principle, private universities must accept more gifted students. The state's function in education should be a supporting role, as it is in the welfare and prison systems."

The Senior Partner at our firm was disturbed by this for several days. Passionate but lacking free time, he suggested I enter politics at the grassroots level. I slouched in my chair at interminable meetings where even students were allowed to denounce the Governor.

When I was asked to give a speech, I found that most enjoyable. I tried to be stirring, but inoffensive. To my surprise, I became Campaign Assistant for our own candidate for Governor, who won. Eight years after that ineffective lie-in on the Capital steps, we finally had power!

Our new Governor—who we had such high hopes for—unfortunately, didn't reduce tuition as we had hoped. He blamed the previous governorship for leaving state finances in a deplorable condition.

During those years, as Assistant to the State Finance Director, I investigated the college Administrative Finance Department. It was a budgetary mess with a shortage of professors. I was surprised to run into George Gross there, then a flunky—some sort of assistant file clerk. I'd always known he wasn't suited for teaching or anything creative. His dud grapefruit was typical of his failures. Even now he hung his head. Still, he obstinately would not tell me what his intentions had been for his orbiting grapefruit satellite. Greasy with failure, his glasses seemed thicker than ever. I consoled him that the Russians had technological failures too. They had landed a whole mining crew against Mars at 25,000 MPH and lost even more men attempting rescues on Venus.

In all honesty, my new administration was having trouble too with finances. Trying to get blood from all those turnips called voters—without enraging them too near election time—required great political acumen. Opinion polls indicated that most voters wished the state college would admit outstanding students and recruit professors with PhDs. So the State Capital increased the college's subsidy, although in principle we looked down on non-self-supporting institutions.

When the college began using income arising from professors' scientific patents to form research and development corporations, our aging Governor, nearing two terms in office, negligently closed his eyes. I worried that those new corporations would compete with free enterprise.

Or create debts the college and state would become legally responsible for, which irate voters would have to rescue them from. When the college began selling stock in their development corporations, I suggested the Governor investigate. Stop this un-American bilking of the public! Now that I was Finance Director, the Governor always listened to me.

I went to see the college Financial Administrator, who surprisingly was George Gross. I warned him that the state would eventually have to bail out his college from financial disaster. Some of the college's foreign corporations had grown too big, already were worth billions. "The bigger they are, the harder they'll fall," I said persuasively.

But Gross informed me that colleges had the best paying lobbyists in the state. I had to pull in my horns, so to speak, and wait for the crash.

Eventually I was elected to the State Legislature, with a new Governor. My small port in a large political storm. This Governor was strangely cooperative with the college, even courteous to professors. I continued in the State Legislature for the next sixteen years, representing the loyal opposition. More soundly than the Governor, I strove for better financial relations between state government and the vast college. When the Legislature postponed a tax increase, the state could not meet its payroll.

George Gross loaned us College Finance Corporation funds at less than their normal interest rate. This good working relationship was, of course, because George and I had been such good friends all our lives. As undergrads thirty-two years ago we had done chicken experiments together, and naturally I had always admired him.

Mr. Gross approved of my political progressiveness, even my ambition for a higher office. Contributions poured into my campaign fund. My post-graduate drama studies at the college had paid off. I won the nomination!

Then one day, thirty-five years after our psychoshock experiments, I suddenly blanked out.

For an instant, I thought I'd died of a stroke, having put on too much banquet-weight campaigning for reelection. Regaining consciousness, I realized that I had not even fallen. I'd simply swayed, as if on an ancient bus. With eyes closed, I imagined staring up at a loudspeaker in an old-fashioned classroom, while a shrill voice, not at all like Mr. Gross's commanding tones, urged us: "Defeat the governor! Abolish tuition. This Day of Infamy must be remembered. We vote this morning. Remember!"

I opened my eyes. By now, most of us old freedom grads were in our late 50s. The women all insisted they were 39. But across the state, we telephoned and organized.

We marched passionately to the Statehouse. We demanded adequate funds for the college. But that sounded strange as we said it because college corporations now owned all the banks. It was the state government that was broke. As if insane, we demanded an end to tuition. But there had been no tuition for twenty years. The college paid all qualified students to attend.

"Student freedom!" we shouted from old memory imprints. Yet outstanding college students were free to sign long-term contracts if they desired college admittance. They could freely give the college their draft rights, to gain lifetime careers in college industries or communications networks. They might even work as Foreign Province Administers.

Student freedom? Were we crazy?

Marching toward the Statehouse as if thirty-five years younger but with arthritic knees, we shouted for college freedom from political interference. But the college controlled the State Legislature. My head throbbed.

Singing ancient freedom songs, we marched up the worn marble steps. Stumbling beside me, George Gross blinked at me through his extra-thick glasses in obvious embarrassment, unable to speak. He too groped up the marble steps as if half blind. Vaguely, I realized that years ago he must have meant to set that timer in his grapefruit satellite for 3.5 years, not 35.

Thirty-five years too late, we stumbled up the steps, near-mummified in ancient memory imprints, shouting, middle-aged, and embarrassed, toward the swinging doors of the state house.

"Vote him out!" my big mouth shouted, as my body struggled up those familiar marble steps. "Defeat the Governor!" I shouted obediently, while inwardly writhing in torment.

I was the Governor.

My reelection now seemed unlikely.

BREAKOUT

A tiny tale written in 1950
Setting: The Future, at Fort Knox

T he General Alarm siren started up with a groan as if it had been sleeping. But by the time Red ran to the door and clicked the magnetic locking mechanism, it had spun itself into a catlike squall. Security forces—machine and man—were deadly quick at Fort Knox.

"No way out, that's what you're saying," Red drawled beneath the angry voice of the siren, then laughed. "But you'll see, you'll see."

Screwing his wide, boyish face into a scowl amidst a galaxy of freckles, he thudded one heavy lead ingot against the steel door. It would take a long time for hydrogen torch flames to spurt through that solid three-inch-thick door.

He'd be the clown no more. For two months he had worked as an assistant manager in the purchasing section, where perpetually giggling typists said he should be on television because he was so funny. But he would be more than funny.

The metallic scrape meant the compound inner gates were opening. That would send frightened jiggles along the pen line of the seismograph normally used to warn of tunneling below. He heard the accelerating clatter of a rising jetcopter, with blades whining. Cordons of interior guards shouted. Some he'd had coffee with; he'd even gone fishing with a few. But they'd blast him now. A dolly-load of lead ingots made the difference.

He grinned. He knew what they were thinking. Nobody can steal an ounce of lead from Fort Knox, much less hundreds of pounds.

The sound of an armored car rumbled into his consciousness. He knew it would advance cautiously, swinging its gun turret like the long nose of a hound midway between two woodchuck scents.

Red hummed to himself, but his trembling gaudy-ringed hands gave him away. He loaded as many ingots as possible onto a dolly, then trundled it up over the edge of the steel plate into Tony's "contraption." Except for the square mouth of its doorway, that invention was featureless as the inside of a Potters Field casket.

Tony had helped him smuggle that contraption in. They had wheeled it right past a sleepy guard, telling him it was a new, secure, lead storage container. After centering it in the ingot storage area, Tony had slipped back out.

Red thought resentfully, *He wants a share of the spoils, but no danger in getting it.* Well no doubt he'd been caught now, was being interrogated. The guard would ask where the guy with Tony had gone. But no one would believe the truth anyway.

It didn't look like that strange looking box could do anything to anybody.

But there was the piebald rat to recall.

Tony—not only an inventor but also a subatomic specialist—had watched that rat for fifteen hours under a low-powered microscope. He then announced that it had regrown with no detriment to the rat. He worked the same trick on an alarm clock.

But as for the clock, Red had put his ear real close. "What's the matter?" he asked. "It ain't tickin'."

Tony hadn't laughed, thinking that must be a significant observation.

S omething clanged against the door. Turning sweaty and scarlet beneath his freckles, Red pulled down a row of heavy circuit-breaker handles. He wished the contraption had a door that could be closed. Officers might break into the room and catch him when he was helpless, no larger than a cockroach.

But he forced himself to relax. He even lit a cigarette before finally pulling the master switch. Exhaling a ribbon of smoke, he heard men hammering on the door. Lots of time. But this was like his first dive from a high board. Would he come up?

" T his is classified info," Tony had said. "But the rat regains its size as the normal bombardment of cosmic rays from the atmosphere knocks electrons loose from their artificially constricted orbits. They spin into their old orbits, disturbing others, freeing them too. The atoms regain their quantum dimensions in an even distribution throughout the rat. So no bodily processes are disarranged as it grows. Even its mental processes appear unimpaired."

Red had nodded, pretending to understand.

Tony had stroked the rat's head with his forefinger. "There is something miraculous about a mammal shrunk to the size of an ant yet come back to nibble on my finger and play like rats do. I wonder if its ego suffered as it got smaller and smaller. Yet it remained its same weight, and strong as ever, even when smaller. Nothing was lost. In fact there was an energy gain, as subatomic bonds were strengthened."

Gain. The cue word. That's what had started Red thinking. Nelda was smiling at astronautics officers again. Handsome, blue-uniformed. Red's jetcopter wasn't enough.

He was the clown and she the queen. But he couldn't risk the rubber-check deal again. His face was too wide and jughead and freckled, too noticeable. After his last try, a druggist had followed him all the way down the street, suspecting his check was bad. He knew his ears stood out in a crowd. Well, forget Nelda. With all this money, maybe he'd find someone better. Younger too.

H is head ached. The steel door was buzzing—perhaps a compressed air chisel cutting the seal. Beyond the square doorway of the contraption, a calendar on the lab wall looked strangely distant. Red hazarded a smile. Soon he would be too small for them to notice him.

I'll push the dolly under the doorsills, around the pebbles. It'll be a long hike. If they step on me, I'll be hard as a tack, a 185-pound tack, a $500,000 tack—that's me. But I gotta watch the time. Eight minutes for a guy my size, Tony said. If I get too small, I'll fall through the molecular latticework.

An extra loud clang made him drop his cigarette. As he bent to pick it up, he wondered why the walls of the contraption hadn't shrunk too. *Maybe that sticky stuff he had me order for it to be painted with? Geez, did I get any on me? I'd shrink unevenly.* Distracted, he picked up his cigarette by the wrong end.

Sucking his burned thumb, he heard a voice over a loudspeaker blaring at him from outside but couldn't make out words. Now the advertising on the calendar was too distant to read, as if he were taking an eye test while backing up. He was shrinking fast, and the dolly of ingots kept pace with him. Yet the walls of the contraption were bare of landmarks to measure himself against, so he found the shrinkage hard to believe.

This deal is easy, he assured himself. *Tony was easy. All we had to do was show fake passes and walk into this vault.*

Now I'm rolling out a dolly-load. What could be easier? He glanced at his watch.

Four minutes to go.

He flinched as the door to the storage room banged inward. It shook the floor like an earthquake, nearly overturning the dolly on his foot. He crouched behind the dolly. Headless giants thundered in, so tall he could only make out giant shoes and calves. Their voices were meaningless as thunder, his eardrums too small to fit the soundwaves. The men didn't seem to notice him. Still, sweating nervously, he glanced impatiently at his watch.

Four minutes to go? Perhaps, in his anxiety, every second simply felt like a minute.

The air was cluttered with spherical things falling soft against his face. Dust, perhaps? His face was hard, dense, a tight grouping of atomic nuclei. The guards became faraway blurs. He looked at the floor of the contraption. Deep pitfalls now surrounded him.

As Red pushed the dolly, it tipped and an ingot slipped out. He leapt after it. Breathing hard, he carried it back. He stared at his watch. Surely he'd been there long enough to shrink to the size he wanted. Why still only four minutes to go?

With horror, he realized that at some point during the shrinking process his watch had stopped.

Gasping, with a flurry of effort, he righted the dolly. He pushed it hard toward the edge of the contraption floor, but before reaching the exit, the dolly veered into a pit.

Moaning, he loaded four ingots in his arms and staggered to the contraption's exit, dropping the ingots over the steep edge of what had now become a cliff.

Lying by the edge of that cliff, he realized he had stopped shrinking. Panicking yet greedy, he ran back to the dolly to save more ingots, leaving dents wherever he stepped. The giants were gone from the supposedly empty room.

He was safe. Now all he had to do was get the dolly unstuck and over that cliff. Then he could get that load out of Fort Knox, right under the door. No one would notice him. Later as his size increased a little, the floor would be smoother. As he grew bigger, he'd move farther and faster. He felt triumphant.

"Nelda, you should've stuck with Papa. When I get money for this lead, I'll be a gentleman of palaces and servants and fur-lined jetcopters with beautiful actresses inside. Beautiful women, and none of them will be you."

An earthquake preceded a shadow. One giant had returned. So what? The ledge bent from Red's weight as he leaned over and looked straight down. He threw his useless watch over, but never heard it strike. Then he remembered the room floor was linoleum layer over concrete. Very porous, full of pits by now. If he dropped more ingots over the edge of the contraption, he might never find them again.

It would take a long time to carry ingots down the cliff, one by one. Then a frightening thought struck him: *What if the guards turn off the lights?* In the windowless darkness he might stumble into a bottomless pit.

He suddenly remembered that once the rat regrew, it grew fast. He too would grow quickly, too large to get under the door and gate. *I've got to act. Better a few ingots than none. I'll start with two, then climb back up the cliff for more if there's time.*

With that, he clutched an ingot under each armpit and stepped off the edge. On the way down, he imagined his ingots impressing Nelda.

But he forgot all as he flashed through the linoleum like a hot needle through butter. Striking feet first, his 185 pounds concentrated on an area no bigger than a needlepoint. Its penetrating force was tremendous as he ripped through huge boulders that composed the concrete floor. Down he plunged, through dirt, through shale, through granite, down toward the center of things.

As friction overcame his momentum, energy he lost in speed was transformed into heat. He screamed in agony. But falling many feet beneath Fort Knox, there was no one to hear him. The smooth pen line of the seismograph proceeded undisturbed.

When his penetration ceased, he was as firmly embedded as a fly in amber. He was nicely preserved, yet still alive, horrified at what he knew would happen next.

That he—inevitably—would grow.

PART THREE: COSMIC ECOPOLITICS

OIL-MAD, BUG-EYED MONSTERS

A short story written in Santa Barbara, CA around 1969
Previously in *Galaxy Science Fiction*
magazine and *Best SF: 1970.*
*Setting: An Oil-Producing Town on the
Pacific Coast, in the Future*

The Pacific Ocean seemed to be burning, adding to the smog. From the upper level of the piggyback freeway, he swerved his little electric car down the offramp to her beach suburb. He glimpsed a fiery finger flickering where the offshore oil drilling platform had stood.

The immense gas flame made him think about a certain nebula. He winced because he had been here now for eighteen years. The flame ought to remind him of something mundane, Earthly, like the gas pilot light in an unlit stove. All the way to the horizon, the ocean was darkening with wasted oil from the undersea gusher.

He swallowed. Waves of oil lapped the beach with gleaming layers like oily—chocolate. The thought made his left stomach rumble hungrily. His right stomach contracted around the olives from uncounted martinis he'd gulped in the metropolitan bar while he was getting her husband's signature on the oil lease.

"She'll never shine...sign," her husband had crooned drunkenly, resting his head on the quaint Mahogany countertop. "You're not man enough to make her. Nobody is."

Legally the couple owned the attractive suburban home in joint tenancy, so he needed her signature, too. He was anxious to rescue the oil underneath their home.

But he felt unsure of his motives. He remembered her huge eyes gleaming with anger. In his loneliness those eyes had appeared as attractively hard as the carapaces of twin black beetles. As beautifully hard-shelled as…his emotions became more confused.

His two hearts beat faster as he drove along her street.

His right stomach squirmed. The alcohol had offered him quick energy but was too insubstantial for his inner organism. It lacked essential hydrocarbons necessary for his innermost distillations. He attempted a grin, but merely grimaced. Here, most humor seemed distorted, an unhappy anomaly, as if these people felt alien on their own planet. So what did that make him? Doubly alien?

At least he was trying to save their oil. He glanced at the sky as if he could see twenty-two more years into the future.

With his wandering thoughts, he accidentally rammed a wooden barricade in the street, then parked. People were evacuating the seashore neighborhood as if they feared an oily holocaust.

He put the half-signed lease in his comfortingly hard-shelled attaché case. On its plastic carapace, with his own daring brand of humor, he displayed new initials in debonair fourteen-carat gold italics: *B. E. M.*

These people seemed stupid, wasting their most vital natural resource. He thought they deserved their future. The woman made him feel altruistic. He wanted to preserve *her* future.

He strolled along the oil-slick sidewalk, inhaling the rich scent of oil. Delicious! Now that he had her husband's signature, she should at least let him inside.

He winked as the sea-breeze sprayed aerosol fine oil droplets against his baby-blue eyes. Rubbing them made his hand shiny as the oil droplets smeared together on his skin. He sneaked a lick.

Yeah!

The estate-type tract house had an embattled look. She had pulled the drapes together. Last Sunday, here on the asphalt driveway, her husband had told him to bug off. But the old bluffer was merely showing off his neighborhood integrity in front of his wife and hulking son.

Today, at high noon in the bar, that old hero had whined: "Neighbors signed. So I'm forced to get mine." His shaking hand had accepted the extra $500 in folded money under the bar. He wouldn't report that to his wife or the IRS. "Now I should buy you a drink, because you won't be able to make her sign. Impossible! You been suckered."

H e knocked on her door. He was afraid he would appear too boyish for her. In his conservative business suit, he still resembled the snub-nosed young radio operator from the oil tanker that had sunk eighteen years ago. Although he had negotiated hundreds of oil leases since then, he still felt hampered by what he saw in the mirror, that young man's startling blue eyes and wispy blonde hair. Even after eighteen years he felt vulnerable without his body-shell.

Across space, separated by light-years from the carapaces of their oil-hungry wives, he and his kind had come. Their little twelve-carapacer had scouted an oil slick. In their excitement they had rammed the tanker, splattering delicious oil. Belatedly they recovered the comatose bodies of its crew. As the youngest Shieldwiper, he had been relegated to the smallest body—that of the young radio operator.

H e imagined the homeowner standing on the other side of her front door, obstinately letting him wait. She was hard-boiled. Then he heard her steel-heeled footsteps. For a moment, his hearts thudded. He pretended he was himself, safely back inside his carapace.

She didn't open the door.

Finally, in frustration, he tapped on it with his attaché case. She and the Smiths were the only ones on this block who hadn't signed. The Smiths were trying to hold him up for more money than their neighbors had received. This one was an idealist, who wouldn't sell out at any price. However, she was human. Was she waiting to get more than the Smiths?

His blonde eyebrows rose as he glanced into her open three-car garage. It contained an outboard motorboat and two empty stalls. He realized the garage might be a clue to her weaknesses. She didn't have a car? Her husband had driven an expensively wasteful gasoline burner to the city. Last Sunday the garage held a four-wheel-drive dune-buggy, with a racing stripe and a high-school parking lot permit on its windshield.

He was surprised such a formidable woman didn't have a car of her own. Apparently both men in her family took advantage of her. This was encouraging.

He smiled. From the corner of his eye, he saw movement through the dining room window. Between the dark drapes, her fiercely beautiful face glared out at him. He nodded, trying to look suave while he opened his hard-shelled attaché case. He held the lease-option up against the glass, confronting her with her husband's signature.

Her expression changed from startled, to pained, to enraged. She looked out at him so haughtily that it reminded him of the gloriously hard face of that Italian actress gleaming through the transparent carapace of his TV. That actress's glittering eyes had excited and disturbed him. He was becoming unwillingly attracted to these angry, soft-shelled ones, but he was so lonely. He sometimes visualized them in invisible, chitinous exoskeletons. He imagined receiving emanations from their gleaming, hardened minds.

He heard the woman's hard heels inside, approaching the front door. He turned again to face it.

The door opened, but not enough. He saw a gleaming security chain. Above it, her eyes glittered. She glared as if he were to blame for the underwater oil gusher and everything else wrong with her world. He felt innocent. Inhuman. For a joyous instant, he felt as if he had regrown his carapace. He felt handsomely shiny, armored with virility. He lowered his attaché case.

"Hi," he said, as if he had forgotten the unpleasantness on Sunday.

Her voice had a hard, resting edge. "I was afraid you'd talk him into—"

"Bought him a Tom Collins," he interrupted brightly, trying to deflect her anger onto her husband. "Slipped him an extra hundred for signing. Oh…I wasn't supposed to tell." He imitated a laugh. Their native games of false truthfulness were as absurdly useful as their humor. "But he's got it."

"Get off our porch."

Her harsh voice made him feel worse than shell-less. In his frustration and loneliness, he felt worse that he was attracted to her. He wanted to remain faithful. He had only 22 more years to wait, but it was difficult.

"I won't sign. Not even if we're the last family on this block."

"You are," he said. "Did your husband telephone you? He told me he would."

"All of you—you're ruining everything."

Her harshness was like a love song. He fought to keep his head.

"I don't have anything to do with that mess." He glanced toward the ocean.

"Believe me, I'm trying to help you save your property values. This oily fog is soaking into my suit. If you'd let me inside—"

"Get out!"

He blinked. He wasn't even in, yet she was telling him to get out. He decided to force entry via his guilt-by-accusation approach. Because they lacked shells, many of these creatures were so vulnerable they acted as if the sins of others were their own. He had noticed they often surrendered to authoritarian or priestly voices.

"You are to blame," he said wildly. "You are all to blame. You didn't try hard enough a year ago when you could have prevented offshore drilling. Now look at what's happened because of self-centered people like you." He added loudly as if broadcasting to her neighbors: "Is it because your husband works for—"

"Shut up. He's not much more than a bookkeeper," she hissed, peeking out of the doorway but not unhitching the chain. "He wasn't involved in any way."

"Oh, but his clients..." he retorted, having no idea whose accounts her husband serviced. "You know as well as I do that their incomes are dependent on transportation, and on other vital parts of the economy that need oil. It's your life blood and mine. Ours?"

He stepped toward her but she started to close the door in his face.

"At least you're not afraid," he said, hurriedly redirecting his approach. "You're not afraid of anything, are you?" he murmured humbly. He pretended she'd defeated him, as if he were no threat to fair womanhood because he was so endearingly boyish and weak. "Could I come inside and rest for a moment?"

"Get off my porch!"

He shrugged, then straightened sternly. Like a process-server, supported by the commanding power of a government, he flashed his lease option. "Better read the fine print."

"I won't sign it."

"Read it." In his business, he had discovered the best way to convince women was to confuse them.

She reached for it. He yanked it away.

"Everyone on your block will get his or her rightful share. Are you too proud to except yours?"

"Mine?" She shrilled, "You've ruined our town."

"Not my company." He hoped a few argumentative maneuvers would lead him into her house. She might let him in while trying to get the last word. He thrust: "You're trying to blame us for wanting to help you."

She retorted, "*You're trying* to force us to permit drilling in our town."

"We want to preserve your natural resources," he explained. "I don't work for an incompetent drilling company. Here, look at our brochure."

"I don't care who you work for."

She pressed outward against the door so the security chain strained.

"Listen," he said. "I care about conservation and decency and freedom. I want to help you save your property value before it drops below what you owe on your mortgage. You don't want to end up with nothing while your neighbors become millionaires."

He pointed across the street. "They've all signed up, except for one old lady who is in Europe but they're still trying to contact her today. If they package that block as a drilling site, we won't need yours. And we won't need your neighbors' lots, with options. Because you waited so long, we can't take up any of our options in this block. Your neighbors' last chance for wealth and happiness will be gone because of you. They'll blame you."

Her eyes glinted, yet she did not unhitch the security chain.

He felt baffled, unable to judge the effect of his greed-fright technique. So he added ominously, "Your block won't even be a truck-parking site if you don't sign. Leasers will tap your oil pool from across the street and toss you a few dollars. They'll paint their derricks green and plant a few trees. They'll park their big trucks where those houses used to be. Your neighbors will have moved away—rich. Oil pumps will be so loud that you won't be able to sleep. No one will buy your house at any price, except me—now."

"We bought our house with rights and covenants. Zoning—"

"It's cracked wide open," he interrupted.

"Your own Town Council is selling the dump for a drilling site, even after the Planning Board designated it as a future park. Our latest survey, since that continuous mess offshore," he jerked his head toward the ocean, "shows that the people know they're licked. Seventy-six percent of voters now favor controlled drilling within the town limits.

"Then the town will begin collecting some oil taxes. Unfortunately, the State and Federal governments have been getting all bonuses and royalties from offshore leases. You've been getting nothing," he finished triumphantly, "except more and more oil on your beach."

"We marched in protest," she blurted.

"And gave up because you know you can't win," he said holding out the lease. "You and your neighbors will be getting fair recompense if you sign this."

She glanced from the maze of small print to his face, then handed the paper back to him. At least she hadn't torn it up. He let his voice smile.

"Now if we could go inside so you can study this…"

"No." But oddly, she laughed. "I could call the police."

"Their telephone number is nine-nine-nine," he said. She shrugged.

Although she did not unchain the door, neither did she close it. He started his penultimate maneuver.

"Your husband said you wouldn't be able to understand any of this anyway."

He turned away but did not put the lease back into his attaché case. He heard a metallic sound and knew it was the door chain.

Her eyes glistened, retreating. He took a deep breath as she let him into the hallway. His human heart thudded as he followed her into the living room.

Sometimes he wondered if the radio operator's body was gradually capturing him. But if so, the female ones should seem beautiful to him. Her grim face was her shield, he thought, but such an inadequate shell. Her resentment and weaknesses seemed nakedly exposed.

"Your husband told me not to tell," he laughed, "which bar I left him in."

Her expression became even more rigid. He established himself on the couch, spreading the pages of the lease option on the coffee table.

"You're wasting your time," she grated, not sitting down. "I won't sign. Where did my husband—"

"It was a dating bar," he said imaginatively. He reached up to switch on a standing lamp to illuminate the splendors of the lease. Its parchment and engraving were the best. "We agree to pay you a thousand a month until we drill. You can't lose a thing, because you keep living here until we pay you twice the property's appraised value as a residence. When this block goes into production, you'll begin receiving your share of royalties and tax advantages, just like the other millionaires."

"What was the name of the bar? He called me from his office."

"You thought." He laughed. "The important thing is— we pay you in stock and stock options. You'll be in the oil business too. You help yourself tax-wise by your share of future exploration expense write-offs.

"You'll even have your own depletion allowance. That's how millionaires are made. Why don't you phone your husband's office? You'll find out he's not there."

"Get out." She glared down at him. "I won't believe anything you say. You're the oil company my husband told me appeared out of nowhere. Fly-by-night."

"Right." He acted as if this were praise—and it was. "Actually, we've been growing for eighteen years. Your husband understands the growth advantages of the oil biz. He knows we've built a beautiful corporate structure. We find oil, pump oil, store oil—we may never need to sell any."

He laughed and what he said was almost true. "As your worth increases, we can issue more stock. Next time you're on the freeway, gaze down at View Pointe street. It overlooks our tank farm."

His human face smiled seductively. "Domestically produced oil has become better than money in the bank, since controls on foreign oil imports. In the interest of national security and to stimulate domestic oil exploration, oil and gasoline prices are rising. By simply storing our oil and never selling any, our company is doing more than its part to improve the price of domestically produced crude.

"Do you follow me? Our oil in storage is constantly increasing in value, so we can issue growing amounts of stock to finance ever-expanding operations. We drill to pump more oil and build more storage tanks, and our growth stocks are like money in the bank—only better."

He saw her weakening, and said, "You see? You understand as much about the oil business as your husband does. Sit down and read the fine print."

"I don't care what you're promising me. There's oil all over our beach."

"Not our oil, "he insisted. "We're very careful about waste."

But she was listening to her feelings instead of his voice.

She murmured, "We moved to this town because it's near the beach. Now it's ruined."

"True," he agreed somberly. "The truth is this town is now ruined as a good place to live. I'm trying to help you save yourself."

"Like rats leaving a sinking ship?"

"We're helping conservation," he replied. "When we buy your house, you'll receive enough money to move to another beautiful town with no underlying oil strata. The value of your stock certificates will keep going up. You must appreciate that we're rescuing oil for future generations."

"That doesn't make sense. Get out."

"By increasing the domestic cost of oil," he pleaded, becoming a supplicant, "we encourage development of better power sources: atomically powered electric generator plants and battery-electric cars."

She huffed. "Then go drill for foreign oil. Allow us to burn theirs, not ours. Get out of our town."

"And let our nation's oil needs become dependent on foreign whims? Our national security—"

"Get out, or I'll phone my husband to throw you out."

He managed to keep a straight human face, though he could not believe she was serious. His voice became soothing.

"Phone him? If you find him, he'll say to sign the lease. He's a man, so he understands that by pumping oil into tanks we're conserving it. He knows irreplaceable oil mustn't be destroyed by fire and end as smog. He knows it should produce more important things, such as petrochemicals and plastics and pharmaceuticals and food."

He didn't know why she was laughing, but her gleaming teeth reminded him of a carapace of glossy chitin. He listened raptly to the harshness of her voice.

"I know what you want." She pointed at the lease. "Get out." Her voice said. "Don't just sit there."

He spread five one-hundred-dollar bills on the coffee table. "No need to tell your husband," he laughed. "Start your own Swiss bank account. Buy yourself a—"

"Get out. What do you think I am?"

She was looking at him instead of the money. He felt confused.

Was her expression from haughtiness or stupidity? Money might be too abstract. She needed something more tangible, he thought.

"Why don't you choose a car," he began. For yourself."

He laughed, seeing her expression. "Your husband and your son race around in theirs, leaving you trapped at home. Listen…you'll look beautiful in a little sports car with your hair streaming in the wind. I'll—we'll—buy you a cute car, your bonus for signing. It'll be yours, all yours."

Watching her grim expression, he described an electric sports car like his own. He spoke with fondness, as if describing a baby.

"I had an accident," she murmured, "a few years ago, but…"

"Electrics are so easy to drive," he said.

"You mean you're only offering me an electric car? Like, thanks—but I don't feel I'm an old lady yet."

"You're quoting oil company propaganda." He laughed. "Not my company. We are financing research for better electrics our subsidiary builds. Ninety miles an hour fast enough for you?"

She squinted. "I thought those weren't allowed on thruways."

"They are this year. We've bought politicians, too." He sobered. "I'll show you my runabout. It's yellow with a vinyl top. You'll have your choice of interchangeable fiberglass bodies."

He spread out a sales brochure. "Cute, huh? Picture your hair streaming back."

"Think of yourself encapsulated," he murmured, "in your cute little car. You'll be giving of yourself patriotically, by conserving irreplaceable oil, while gliding electrically, soundlessly, and smoglessly." He paused for a long, quivering breath. "While future generations revere you."

He had been told that whatever he said to women during his sales pitch was less important than the tone of his voice. "Your oil is too wonderful to be burned while millions starve. Sign here, if you believe in conservation. The anciently formed molecules of oil must not be burned, because millions of years are needed for oil to be born again. Oil doesn't regenerate during one man's lifetime like a pine forest. It can't renew itself every year like a field of wheat. Yet it can provide protein for the starving—that is, bacteria that feed on oil—an intermediate step."

He sighed, moving nearer to her. "Anaerobic bacteria, needing no air, can feed deep in the earth. They sometimes clog oil wells. Here's my pen."

He moved closer. "You'll save oil for starving babies. On the surface, airy-aerobic-bacteria can be fed oil, if air and moisture are bubbled through with infinitely small quantities of salts essential to growth. How fast they grow! Every pound of aerobic bacteria multiplies so fast each day, it produces ten more pounds of nutritious protein. Lives of millions of malnourished children can be strengthened if you'll sign on this line."

He grimaced, inwardly hating children, and feeling that anaerobic and aerobic bacteria were equally disgusting little competitors. Much less efficient than he was—but at least their oil wasn't wasted as smoky exhaust fumes. These people were insane!

He watched her unpleasantly flexible fingers moving the pen, then barely touched the distressing softness of her arm.

"Hey! What's the matter with you?" She lurched up from the couch, then laughed uneasily. "Am I supposed to be flattered or feel grateful at my age? You're…don't get any ideas, just because you've promised to buy me a car."

Her eyes gleamed confusingly as he, too, rose. It seemed as if she were encased in transparent chitin. She sidled away, trying to watch him while she lit a cigarette with trembling hands. Although he flinched from the flash of flame, her silvery lighter made him think of a beautifully metallized carapace so he advanced. The proper approach would be a couple of quick symbolic taps of his carapace against hers.

But she dodged and seemed ready to scream. He realized he had better start with a ritual more familiar to her. Whichever way he twisted his head as she backed away, his lips were confronted by the dangerously hot tip of her cigarette.

She suddenly shoved him, elbowing his unshielded right stomach. He felt a hydrogen gas bubble rise from his earlier conversion of martinis. Like a balloon, it pressed against his throat bi-way valve. For an instant he feared ignition from her cigarette. As he turned his head away to belch discreetly, she ducked under his arm and escaped through the dining room and into the kitchen. He followed her, muttering apologies. She jerked open a drawer and grasped something attractively metallic.

"Keep away," she gasped.

Was he seeing a steely-bright carapace, or was that a stainless-steel carving knife in her human hand? He clacked inquiringly, feeling invulnerable to the potential thrust of steel into his handsomely gleaming shell. But if he turned out not to be knife-proof the autopsy would expose everything.

It would be twenty-two more years before the breeding fleet could arrive in this solar system. They had removed his carapace surgically. Concealed in seamen's bellies, he and the other eleven had managed to infiltrate this outrageous world. They had seen its shell-less bipeds squandering irreplaceable oil. Oil had to be saved for posterity—his. Pooling the first major earnings of their new identities, all twelve had bought oil stocks. They had operated shrewdly. When they had learned more about being men, they leased desert land, issued stock, and joy and calamity, struck oil.

They were trying to save oil, not sell it. The answer was the tank-farm gimmick. While paying for more storage tanks by issuing growth stocks, they discovered tax angles, including purchasing an electric car manufacturing company to acquire its paper losses.

By this time, the other eleven had become remote chairmen of boards of directors. Because he was the only one continuing direct contact with the public as a lease-man, the unfriendly eleven accused him of un-shell-like urges. They were afraid he might crack before they controlled the whole planet's oil before the breeding fleet arrived. They said he took human risks, even driving on the freeway. If he were killed in an accident, his autopsy might lead to their exposure.

Still, he cornered this woman between the gleaming dishwasher and the glittering refrigerator. She gasped, "Don't look at me like that."

But suddenly her carving knife clattered to the floor. She said, "I can't do it. I can't stick you like a pig. So kiss me if that's what you're trying to do."

With his eyes closed he tried. She was so soft—the opposite of truly armored love, so … so horribly soft. He shrank back in normal revulsion. He opened his eyes. She had no shell at all. She opened hers.

He fled through the house to the living room and he snatched up his reassuringly hard attaché case. To his dismay, she followed.

Smiling oddly she said, "What about my car…"

He gasped and grabbed the lease from her coffee table. "I'll authorize delivery of it." Desperately he rushed outside. He scuttled along the slippery sidewalk toward the shell-like security of his car. He felt so humiliated.

He tried to assure himself that her signature on the lease was the only important thing. He had that. But tears trickled down his hideously human cheeks.

At least he had secured another drilling site, he thought, as he drove ninety miles an hour along the freeway. Twenty-two more years to wait. He pounded his forehead against the glinting steering wheel. His car swerved. He turned into the parking area above View Point, as if the sight of his oil tanks could give him some relief.

He parked at the brink and tried sublimating, pouring himself an abstemious reward for getting her signature. With trembling hands, he opened yet another can of adequate little 30-weight, non-detergent oil and sipped, attempting to restrain himself. Then he drank desperately. But the act only stimulated his loneliness.

He looked up at the empty gray sky, then glared out at the ocean, dark with wasted oil. At least he was more intelligent than humans. He glanced into his car's mirror at his obscenely huge blue-eyed reflection.

Eventually he regained his poise. He knew who he was. He felt armored again, secure and restrained. He knew he could wait twenty-two more years for his wife and the breeding fleet. His gaze shifted between the oil-blackened ocean, jagged with human drilling platforms, and those bulging mad-blue eyes in the mirror.

He felt thankful he wasn't human.

TO GRAB POWER

A short story written in 1970
Previously in *IF Worlds of Science Fiction, 1971*
and an anthology edited by Isaac Asimov
Setting: A recreated instaplanet

O n the next downtrip, while the short-winged shuttle skimmed through the man-made atmosphere high above the instaplanet's rain-filled meteoritic craters, someone fell out.

Or so it appeared, on the luminescent screen in the dark stone hut—like a falling spark, falling like a shriek. The young bodyguard stared at it with surprise and horror.

Falling before the shuttle's radar blip, the spark seemed too big to be a man. But perhaps a man's arms and legs were spread in the thickening air, in an attempt to resist the inevitable.

"Is he conscious?" cried the old man's voice in the hut.

"Maybe if he had time to close his helmet." The bodyguard's boyish face became wide-eyed as he imagined himself falling toward the instaplanet with its meteor-pocked surface glittering with thousands of crater-ponds like new coins.

Air-drops had planted fish in them. But for some reason, all the villages still crowded around one vast polluted lake where a little volcanic island muddied the clouds with smoke.

The spark approached the island.

"He's falling through the air too fast, getting too hot." The bodyguard's broad forehead wrinkled. "… unless he's in an escape bag with an ablative foot cone."

From the bottom of the screen rose the volcano's image. The bodyguard's heart pounded. One of his greatest desires was to enter its smoldering crater to search for the forbidden weapons rumored to be hidden there.

"No parachute opened," he said as the spark faded into the radar-confusing smoke. "I guess he wasn't in an escape bag. But whatever he was in made an awful big blip on the screen." His youthful gestures were lightning quick, manipulating the screen. "Look, there's the shuttle, following its usual landing spiral back toward our end of the lake. So, it couldn't have been the pilot who fell out."

A gust of rain lashed through the crevices in the crude stone hut.

"It must've been Henrydavid," the old man moaned, leaning forward until his jagged face was silhouetted against the screen. His bodyguard looked away in embarrassment at the rough stone wall that was weeping rain. To him the old man had long seemed such a strong source of power, almost too unsubstantial to grasp.

The old man asked, "Do you think this is another attempt by those unforgiving Centralist exiles?"

"More likely an accident in the shuttle," his bodyguard said. "But you'd better go back to the village." The young man took a deep breath. "I'll paddle out to meet the shuttle."

"No…" the old man said uncertainly.

Without replying, the bodyguard darted out under smoky sunlit-edged clouds. He was uncomfortably short, but no one taunted him anymore because of his wide shoulders. After his strange battle on that volcanic island, he'd been asked by the old man to be his bodyguard. He had agreed back then because he was restless, born restless, wanting to be near power. As a small boy he had dreamed of becoming so big he filled the universe with his power.

Now looking up at the rainbow-arched sky, he felt tall. He remembered Henrydavid, not falling through the air, but in the past standing lithely against the inside the shuttle as it clung to a synchronously orbiting freighter. Aluminum shield supply containers as big as caskets were shoved in through the flexible iris that was its hatch. Henrydavid's job as customs inspector was—or had been—to open them immediately.

With mixed emotions, the bodyguard frowned. The old man wanted to prevent Centralist propaganda from reaching the instaplanet via the shuttle. But certain young men here wanted it…

"We'll both go out to meet the shuttle," the old man said, lifting one end of the heavy greenish canoe.

The bodyguard had shaped it by hand-pressing layers of filamentous algae over the hull of an existing canoe. Once firmed up, he had smeared it with fish oil and dutifully baked it in the sunlight. But the old man didn't know he had cheated a little. He'd also baked it in the village's hydrogen fusion-powered electric oven. The wooden paddles had been imported from Earth.

As the crude canoe slashed out on the immense lake, the water became lively with raindrops and minnows. He had been taught that the lake and the countless crater-ponds had been filled by the Great Rain ten years before he was born on this instaplanet. Before that, the supersaturated air had been produced by remolecularly rising rocks from both poles. After the air had become sweet and the rains diminished, the planet had been planted with life. The old man and his followers had then been delivered to it as an experiment.

Economic or Philosophic? The bodyguard wondered what kind of world it would become.

Now the greenish lake swirled, as great fish devoured each other in richly putrefying jungles of algae. But the land had remained barren rock, as clean and simple as the Decentralist ideal.

In the bow of the canoe, the old man moved his paddle with slender back and arms but quiet grace. In the stern, his young bodyguard paddled with driving force. Between the two, a mustache of foam pushed from the blow as their canoe approached the shuttle.

For the bodyguard, the shuttle carried the exciting power of Earth, where he wanted to go. Its heat-stained hull contained beautiful steel tools, bright mirrors, and colorful beads. He had heard fabulous tales of Earth weapons with wonderful thunder-and-lightning power which could be held in a boy's hand. He had decided the shuttle to the freighters was the one contact with Earth which must never be broken, no matter what the old man preached.

"Now it's killed someone," the old man blurted, as the canoe surged threateningly close to the shuttle's scarred hull.

But his bodyguard smiled with excitement. The shuttle contained power that could be physically grasped. Already concealed in his kirtle of woven algae was his most wonderful possession: a steel dagger, smuggled from Earth. If the old man had known he had it, he would have told him to throw it overboard because it was a weapon, as was any knife more than three inches long.

The old man would have said, "Weapons lead to uncontrollable power, to Centralism. Beware."

The bodyguard scowled at the straight old back as they drifted alongside the shuttle. Respectful people in the villages still addressed the old man as Mr. Decentralist. Some had shortened this to Mr. Decent. But the restless young laughed bitterly. It was their fathers who had brought Decentralism to this instaplanet.

Now young men paced the barren rocks and looked out at the volcanic island, remembering Big Village before its fall. They stared at the forbidden island, dreamed of another central city, and cursed the old man behind his back.

The bodyguard laid down his paddle and picked up his trident fish-spear. His clumpy algal canoe bumped the marvelously complex shuttle. Without its usual hiss of air pressure, the shuttle's hatch opened like a camera-eye. Its inner iris looked rubbery.

The pilot's oddly blank face protruded.

"It wasn't my fault," The shiny arm of his metallicized suit flew up. "...that your customs inspector was blown out like that! The valve popped off the emergency air tank and air pressure did the rest. I always said that valve was dangerous. It was poorly designed."

Or sabotaged, the bodyguard thought as he scrambled into the shuttle. For this downtrip, in the hold he saw no unannounced passengers. He eyed the rows of long aluminum supply containers, which they received from Earth in exchange for their little bottles of fish-gland extracts. Whenever he had entered the shuttle, it had had this fishy smell.

"So, the air pressure shot up in here," the pilot reexplained, his jowls quivering.

The young bodyguard remembered Mr. Decentralist's warning that such stocky or obese men were apt to be unfaithful to Decentralist ideals. It was true that the most dedicated Decentralists, who lived with austerity and simplicity, had naturally narrow physiques like Mr. Decent. The bodyguard frowned. He didn't trust this pilot.

The man continued to bluster. "I always said this loading iris is too flexible. All that pressure bulged it out, blew him out."

"Did Henrydavid have time," Mr. Decentralist asked hopelessly, "to close his helmet visor?"

"Don't know. I had to hang onto the control panel." The pilot shifted his gaze from the old man's jagged face to the bodyguard's blunt expression of disbelief.

"Why," the bodyguard challenged, "weren't any of these containers blown up with him?"

"Because he'd already inspected them and strapped them down again," the pilot answered, "for landing as usual. Anyway, they're too streamlined to be sucked out."

The bodyguard felt outsmarted. He quibbled. "This one isn't strapped tight."

He knew the customs inspector had been a conscientious man who would have tightened the strap if he'd had time. He deliberately pointed his fish-spear, defined as a tool, not a weapon, toward the pilot's abdomen. "Did Henrydavid have time to open all the containers?"

"Yes, he always does—open them," the pilot blurted. He looked to Mr. Decent. "I feel bad about this."

"I think we'd better inspect them again," the bodyguard said.

"Not now," replied Mr. Decent. "We've got to search for Henrydavid." The bodyguard blinked with surprise.

The pilot also stared at Mr. Decent.

"We wouldn't be able to find anything," the pilot explained. "The shuttle was moving so fast when he was blown out, his descent speed so great, his body must have burned in the atmosphere."

The bodyguard checked the emergency rack's twelve cubicles, where glittering, heat reflective escape bags lay. At the bottom of each were ablative cones, for casting off flame as the bags penetrated the atmosphere. At the tops were two-stage parachutes. All twelve were still in the rack. No bags were missing.

The bodyguard scowled, feeling baffled.

"He wasn't falling that fast," he argued. "In a safety suit like yours, his body wouldn't burn very much."

"You don't understand anything," the pilot retorted, "about atmospheric entry speed. It would have burned him to a crisp."

"You're the expert," Mr. Decent murmured to the pilot, "but I know we must recover his body."

"It was burned to ashes," the pilot insisted. He added, too gently, "He often said he'd want to go this way, with his ashes scattered over the lake he loved so well. There's no use searching for his ashes. He would have wanted it this way."

Enough lies, the bodyguard thought. He was now convinced that the shuttle's speed had been reduced by the time Henrydavid was "blown out." The body couldn't have burned to ashes. But he didn't want to look for it either. Was this "accident" a decoy or a trap?

But he was so angry he said, "I know his suit will have preserved most of his body. We'll start searching near the island."

"Near Big Village?" The pilot protested. "For his ashes?"

"Yes, in the water around the volcano," the bodyguard replied. He noted the pilot's unhappy face. "Did you know we were watching the radar screen when it happened?"

The pilot glanced at Mr. Decent. "It would be too dangerous for you—for anyone—to go over there in a canoe."

"Too slow," the old man said. Then his voice broke: "Henrydavid may be alive... floating, drowning..."

"He means rush us over there now, in this shuttle," the bodyguard said.

The pilot protested. "Using a space shuttle like a canoe—"

"That's what we've always used it for," the bodyguard interrupted, "...when no freighters have been in orbit. Push the REFUEL button."

Gurgling, the shuttle refilled its water tanks. That technique was frequently employed to distribute supplies to other villages along the lakeshore. The pilot should know that.

"Now pull the FUSION lever, but only to the first mark." The bodyguard had ridden in the craft several times, though he'd only been as far as the freighter orbit. He knew the shuttle merely needed steam now, not disassociated hydrogen and oxygen flaring to hurl them into space. "We're only going around Volcano Island."

A humming sound came from the shuttle's bowels, where the magnetic bottle, containing its hydrogen fusion, produced heat. There was hissing as water turned to steam, then a roar from the dual-purpose thruster. The shuttle surged across the wide lake, steam billowing behind its high-finned tail.

"Look at that little canoe over there," the bodyguard shouted. He was surprised and suspicious, as it seemed to be headed toward the forbidden island. Its paddlers noticed the shuttle's course. As if having guilty consciences, they turned back to the mainland.

The volcanic cone squatted on the contorted rim of a half-drowned meteor crater. The bodyguard knew this lone volcano had burst from a crack while the planet was being distorted by the remolecularization of rock from its polls. The crater had cooled while he was still a boy. But smoke rose from a recent split.

He knew the main reason people with Centralist tendencies had established a village beside the cone, upon the meteoric rim enclosing the harbor. It was to tap the volcano's heat for use in illegal manufacturing. They had begun making metal forks and spoons—and sharper things the bodyguard secretly wished he could own. Daggers. Even more powerful weapons.

Centralists were never satisfied, he thought. And now their village was deserted. Wonderful things had been thrown into the lake. His visualization of those beautiful lost weapons made his heart pound with desire. He wanted again, on this errand, to search the crater for unfinished weapons, but the old man was along. The bodyguard glared toward the mainland.

"There's another canoe," the bodyguard shouted harshly. "See? Coming from that new village—a long dark canoe?"

It didn't seem intimidated by the shuttle. The bodyguard thought it might be headed for the island. Or its dozen paddlers might simply be loyal Decentralists, going fishing. He remembered that some Centralists had dispersed along the shore, adjacent to the new village, after Mr. Decent had ordered Volcanic Island evacuated.

While the shuttle cruised near the island, the bodyguard watched for telltale gulls. But they saw no sign of the customs inspector's body.

"Go into the harbor," Mr. Decentralist said unexpectedly.

The bodyguard's heart thudded as they entered the harbor's rocky jaws. Big Village clung to the cliffs, deathly silent, empty-eyed stone huts staring at him. He felt both guilt and pride. He clutched his fish-spear as if it were a weapon. It was here he had shown he was a man.

One gull fluttered up from the water, but it had been feeding on a big dead fish. This volcano above Big Village had polluted its harbor even more than its air. He winced, yet felt nostalgia. He remembered Big Village that day when it had been alive with runaway girls singing and illegal forges clanging.

He was then a youth in the angry armada of paddlers from little villages cautiously approaching this Centralist stronghold. He had felt awe and envy, seeing how rich in populace Big Village had become. There were more than two hundred huts. Centralists had crowded the stone dock. His heart had leaped on seeing three Supreme Weapons glinting in the sunlight.

Now he scowled, peering down at the dark, deep water of the harbor.

Mr. Decent's cried out, "Look, up there!"

A blade of sunlight illuminated a tiny red stain on the volcano's flank, high above the dead village. The old man moaned, "Henrydavid…"

Both realized their falling customs inspector had struck the planet like a meteorite. The bodyguard's gaze rose to the lip of the crater. He tried to suppress his desire to enter it. This wasn't a good time, although the rim was only a few minutes climb above the red splash of Henrydavid.

"I've got to go up," Mr. Decent said sadly. "Henry, oh, Henry."

The bodyguard argued that it was forbidden to land on the island. "You made the rule. Anyway, this might be a trap."

But the distraught old man ordered the pilot to bring the shuttle alongside the algae-shrouded stone dock.

"That canoe may get here soon," the bodyguard warned.

"They may be coming because they saw him fall."

There was no use arguing with the old man. Also, unless the wind changed so the paddlers could open their sailing umbrellas, the bodyguard knew the canoe couldn't get there for at least an hour. As he followed the old man onto the dock, his own desire rose.

Then he slipped on algae and recovered his natural alertness. He jumped back aboard the shuttle before the pilot could escape and backed the man toward one aluminum container.

"Open it. Now dump out those pamphlets. Pamphlets? Anyway get in. You won't smother. The lid doesn't fit that well." He tightened the straps. "Don't go away," he said, clambering out on the shuttle's deck.

He tied the shuttle fast to a stone cleat on the dock, then ran after the old man through the crumbling village of memories.

Years Before

T he Armada approached Big Village, which illegally contained at least a thousand people. The maximum permissible size for a community on this instaplanet was a hundred. Big Village was a fabulous place; young runaways had flocked to it. One young man in the Armada smiled with excitement, rather than fear, at seeing three gleaming supreme weapons. Those rested in the hands of the most important men in Big Village. But they were only fat, middle-aged men.

Mr. Decent boldly landed on the dock to negotiate or accuse. "You've taken nuke boxes from five villages, depriving them of electricity."

"You old hypocrite," the mayor of Big Village retorted. "You complain about us taking electricity, while urging decentralization of people into groups of tens—or families— to live without electricity. Look. We have so many people here who need it, we need ten electric-boxes, not five. Earth sends a box to this planet for each hundred people. So, we have the right to proportional allocation of electric power."

"No." Mr. Decentralist shook his head. You're rebuilding all the confusion and greed we tried to leave behind on Earth." He shouted, seeing the glinting knives, "You're even manufacturing inhumane weapons." He rashly grabbed at one but fell during the ensuing scuffle. His shrill fellow Decentralists scrambled from canoes to the dock, thrusting out their fishing spears like weapons.

"Defense!" the mayor had yelled over his shoulder. His own men rushed to deflect fish-spears with aluminum shields. They raised those three beautiful steel weapons.

Blades flashed in the sunlight, but the young man who hoped he'd someday be a bodyguard, felt no fear—even as the Centralists attacked. Instead of fleeing, he circled one, until that Centralist slipped on blood and fell, his supreme weapon clanging against the stones.

The young man rushed forward and wrested away the sword. It was now his. He tightly gripped its hilt and dodged a thrust from the second swordsman. With youthful quickness he swung his great blade back and forth, striking his opponent's neck. Now he had the knack of it, the bodyguard-to-be rushed at the third middle-aged man. Around him the excited Decentralists had attacked with their fish-spears.

The Big Villagers scattered, ending the battle abruptly. Thus began the problem of what to do with so many defeated people who were still Centralists at heart.

N ow, years older, the bodyguard ran through the empty village after the old man. If the wind changed, the long canoe might approach rapidly, possibly filled with Centralist renegades.

On one side of the volcano, he saw Mr. Decent kneel in grief by a great red splash with Henrydavid's fragmented safety suit.

The bodyguard hurried past him, saying he was climbing higher looking out for the canoe. But there was another reason.

From the rim of the volcano, he looked out over the immense wind-wrinkled lake and the lonely land beyond. Countless crater-ponds glittered, where the old man wanted people to spread out in smaller groups for a simpler way of life.

The bodyguard smiled and shook his head. That long dark canoe was still a long way off. Whether it contained faithful Decentralist fisherman or unrepentant Centralist rebels, they still paddled against the wind. He might have time to search the crater.

He peered down into the dark funnel, heart pounding as it had when he had seized the sword in the battle of Big Village. The greatest disappointment of his life had come after the fighting. The old man had honored him by choosing him to be his bodyguard, but then made him throw all three swords into the lake. The now-bodyguard had secretly returned later to dredge unsuccessfully for them, cursing and crying because he had stupidly thrown away their power.

No unfinished swords had been found in Big Village, so he thought an illegal weapons forge might be concealed in this crater. As he descended, he wrinkled his nose at the sulfurous stench. He began searching under lava ledges for even one unfinished sword.

His eyes widened. Below him, near a vertical split where steaming rainwater drained out of the crater, he saw something white and rumpled. He clutched his fish spear like a weapon and clambered down, sending rocks rattling.

The whiteness was a folded parachute, partially covering an escape bag. Except for its ablative foot cone, the bag lay flat. It was a different model from the twelve in the shuttle, open and empty. No one was on the nearby rocks. The inspector must have fallen out before landing. But why would he have been in an escape bag descending into the crater?

Anyone peering out through the bag's periscope could have steered its chute away from or toward the volcano, while breathing from its oxygen tank. But what reason would Henrydavid have for descending from the shuttle in an escape bag?

He clutched his spear and looked around quickly, but still saw no one crouching in ambush among the rocks.

"Don't move," a hoarse voice suddenly said.

The parachute cloth squirmed, and a swollen-faced middle-aged man emerged from under it. He held a gleaming metal rod with a round hole in its end, pointed at the bodyguard. He sat up, and said, "Throw away your spear—that's right."

The bodyguard's heart was again drumming with excitement rather than fear as he stared at this ultimate weapon. It could change life on his instaplanet. Its barrel and folding stock gleamed with the promise of power. One of the man's hands gripped its long bullet clip while the other enclosed its trigger mechanism.

"Stop smiling," the man shrilled, as if in great pain. "Who are you?"

"A fisherman," the bodyguard finally answered. He was surprised the man didn't recognize him from the Battle of Big Village or its aftermath. "I just climbed here to—"

"Don't move. I'll shoot." The parachutist grimaced, then looked disappointed. "Don't you know who I am?"

"No," the bodyguard lied.

He now glimpsed the brilliant scheme by which this exiled mayor of Big Village hoped to re-enter the instaplanet undetected. As for the falling spark on the radar screen— anyone familiar with the operation of the shuttle would reason it to be the customs inspector falling alone from some accident. But Henrydavid had not fallen alone. The pilot was part of the conspiracy,

The bodyguard imagined the scene inside the shuttle after leaving the freighter with containers. He guessed that the pilot struck Henrydavid on the head. Then no doubt this blotchy-faced man had emerged from one container then pulled his special escape bag from another. He could have tied Henrydavid's body to the outside of this bag using parachute control lines. After arranging the bag against the hatch iris, the Centralist ex-Mayor must have sealed himself inside it and waited.

The bodyguard's eyes widened in admiration. When the shuttle had approached the smoke from the volcanic island, the pilot must have knocked the valve off the reserve air tank. That sudden increase in air pressure had blown the flexible iris outward, hurling the escape bag into space. That would have made it fall diagonally toward the island, appearing on their radar screen as a single spark. No wonder it had seemed surprisingly large for one man.

The bodyguard smiled at this fabulous ex-Mayor. He must have yanked the extra control line at the last moment, freeing himself from the weight of Henrydavid's body. He then could have guided the escape bag into radar-confusing smoke—undetectable on the radar—then deployed the drogue chute. Finally, opening his main chute he had skillfully steered it to disappear in this volcanic crater.

Yet the man seemed to have broken his leg. It had an unusual bend to it.

"Let me help you—to climb out of here," suggested the bodyguard.

"Keep away."

The gun barrel rose. The Centralist's thick body shifted, and his face contorted in pain.

The bodyguard nodded obediently, awaiting his chance. His gaze again devoured the beautiful gun. It was the first he had seen, other than in smuggled pictures.

"Is that a sub-machine gun?"

"You don't even know who I am," the middle-aged man exclaimed angrily. "You don't know what to do."

The bodyguard considered the dagger concealed in his kirtle. Whipping that out would take too long. "Let me help, or you'll die down here. "Look, there's blood leaking where your leg-zip is open on your suit. A compound fracture?"

"Stay back," the man rasped. "I don't need you. Others are coming to this island to meet me."

"In canoes?" The bodyguard feigned surprise. He doubted the man could have seen the long canoe through his periscope while the bag descended. "There aren't any canoes out there, except mine. So, you need my help. I've always wanted the good things they have on Earth. I wish

I'd been born there—with all the autocars, and television boxes, and great cities …"

Attempting to sound like a Centralist, his voice grew so convincing that what he said became true. He did want what the Centralists wanted, and he also wanted the gun. He saw the barrel lowering as the parachutist's arms relaxed. Soon he could grab it, the new ultimate weapon on the instaplanet.

Rocks rattled behind him. He whirled. In the distance, a scrawny figure clambered down from the rim.

"Who's that?" The parachutist hissed.

"Another fisherman," the bodyguard lied hopelessly.

"Wave to him to come down." Evidently the Centralist thought he needed two to carry him.

"He's coming," The bodyguard hoped the old man would see the gun and run. Mr. Decent had upset his plan before he could execute it—before he could somehow grab the gun and hide it to return for later. But Mr. Decent must see it and would of course make him drop it into the lake. The bodyguard scowled.

The old man was scrambling down, clutching a bloody scrap of cloth as if it were all that was left of Henrydavid.

"You!"

"You! Don't come any closer." The ex-Mayor shifted the gun between the bodyguard and the old Decentralist. "I'll shoot you, you old hypocrite."

"You agreed not to return," growled Mr. Decent. The wind wailed above the crater. "Why are you here?"

The bodyguard saw volcanic smoke rising across the sky and realized the wind had changed. Those in the canoe, fisherman who might be Centralists, would open sailing umbrellas and surge toward the island. The bodyguard couldn't wait much longer.

While he watched for a chance to leap at the gun, he felt strong and quick, like when he had dodged those sword thrusts at that battle. He supposed a bullet wouldn't be much faster than a sword. It was such a little thing. The round eye of the gun muzzle stared back at him.

"Move back," the ex-Mayor said, "Closer to Mr. Decentralist."

The bodyguard smiled and didn't move. He silently willed Mr. Decent to not mention the long canoe. The ex-Mayor would assume it carried the Centralist activists to meet him. He would feel free to squeeze the trigger, shooting the old man. But the bodyguard couldn't conceive himself being killed. He leaned toward the Centralist leader, waiting for his opportunity.

"You can't be Mayor of an empty village," Mr. Decent bargained. "I let you go before. I'll let you go back to Earth again."

"Hypocrite!" the ex-Mayor cried. "You talked of peace and individual freedom, then you led the attack on Big Village. You would have been kinder had you executed me then. This is my island. Where are my people now?"

"Dispersed," the old man retorted. "Enjoying pure and simple lives again."

"He's a fanatic," the Centralist hissed frantically to the bodyguard, "a fanatic old man. He thinks a hundred people are too many for a village. He wants to disperse families, one to a pond—and after that what?"

"Transcendent freedom," the old man replied, "to contemplate."

"Freedom to isolate yourself beside a pond," the centralist cried, "on a bare planet? To think about what? You hypocrite! Already in your little villages there is no freedom for young people to do what they want to do, which is to get together and—"

"They're growing up unspoiled." Mr. Decent looked to his young bodyguard, who realized that both, the old man and the middle-aged man, Decentralist and Centralist, were now speaking to him rather than to each other.

"This old man is trying to be a mental jailer for you young people. Listen!" The parachutist obviously wanted his help and allegiance.

Each seemed to be trying to win him, to use him. As if he represented all young people on this planet, its future.

The wounded Centralist insisted: "It's this old man's fault your instaplanet is tied to an unfair economic plan. That damned plan for economic decentralization was written by bureaucrats on Earth, to benefit Earth. That's why we weren't allowed to manufacture anything. That's why villages were limited to a hundred people. In that inhumane plan, all we're supposed to do is catch fish and send their glandular extracts to Earth. Listen, unless we centralize, our instaplanets' unfavorable balance of trade will keep us poor colonial slaves."

"Who needs trade?" the old man retorted. "Good Decentralists are learning to do without Earth's corrupting products. We have fish and health-giving algae. We can weave kirtles and build stone shelters. We can be free of Earth trash. We don't need that accursed shuttle anymore. We don't have to rely on Earth."

"That's right," the Centralist interrupted. He smiled wryly at the young man. "When we have a great industrial city, we won't have to rely as much on Earth. We can enjoy—"

"—polluting our lives!" Mr. Decent shouted. "We came here to escape evil, noise, and greed. We accepted that economic plan so Earth would pay our transportation here."

The parachutist nodded. He stared at the bodyguard while replying. "Yes, after the Bureau of Colonization created air and water on this planet, it wrote our unfairly limited Economic Plan so we'd always be dependent on them."

He grimaced with pain, trying to move his leg. "It contradicted our Constitution," he added bitterly.

"You signed the plan, though," the old man said.

"So did you. I was younger than you and innocent then," the middle-aged parachutist retorted. "You hypocrite! You signed the Economic Plan, but in your own way you're trying to be free of it too.

"You tell villagers to forget their material needs, to stop sending fish extracts to Earth. You claim we will be free of Earth if we scatter to isolated ponds. To philosophic idiocy. But most of us want to build a great city, to create our own independent industries. That's the way to be free of Earth."

The ex-Mayor looked hopefully at the young man, who only stared mutely at the gun.

But he was listening. The bodyguard wished the Decentralist and Centralist could agree that, beyond the need for independence from Earth, each group could follow its own desires. Including him, wanting that gun.

"Give up," the old man demanded. "Give up the gun."

"Hypocrite!" the Centralist cried. "It was you who used force against us. First you old hypocrites tore out the last page of our Constitution, so you could feel free to attack us. You tore out the right to assemble, to choose a way of life, to build a city. All that was in our Constitution, until you old men became so terrified you tore it out. You stole freedom from our young people."

He looked at the young man. "Our Constitution, written on Earth, was above the Economic Plan. Ask this old man what happened to its last page."

The young bodyguard was vaguely aware of a weathered copy of the Constitution on display in his village. But he had never gotten around to reading it. He shrugged.

"The majority of village elders voted to remove the last page," Mr. Decent said weakly. "It was necessary to defend our villages from you."

"That wasn't the reason!" the Centralist gasped.

"It was," Mr. Decent retorted. "We can't permit violations of Decentralism which would seduce our young people. We can't permit corruptions such as Big Village, if our way of life is to survive. You criminal, you murderer!" The old man pointed a finger red with the blood of his customs inspector. "You murdered Henrydavid, didn't you?" He shivered violently with rage.

The bodyguard expected Mr. Decent to leap at the Centralist ex-Mayer, who might shoot him. And if he did? That might be his opportunity to grab the gun, all its power!

"Give it to me." The old man stepped toward the ex-Mayor, reaching out for the gun as if simply dealing with another young, decentralized villager. "I say, give it to me."

As the gunman's tendons tightened, the bodyguard saw he did intend to shoot, to kill Mr. Decent. The bodyguard lunged faster than thought possible, in a conditioned reflex called duty, as he grabbed the barrel to yank it aside. A hammer slammed his chest so hard he fell backward. He felt a terrible burning, yet the rocks seemed soft.

He hadn't expected this. Hadn't he wanted the old man—the old order—to die? Instead, he had saved Mr. Decent's life. His hand wrapped around the warm smoothness of the gun barrel. As he sat up, he was amazed at how much his chest hurt when he coughed, blood spattering. He wanted to say something.

"You've shot him!" Mr. Decent yelled distantly. "He's dying."

Through dizzily fluctuating light and darkness, the bodyguard saw the ex-Mayor crawling toward him, dragging a broken leg, reaching to retrieve the gun.

"Shoot, shoot," the old man shouted.

The bodyguard's numbed fingers groped at the trigger as he saw Mr. Decent hurl himself upon the ex-Mayor. Through his blurring vision and the crazy darkness in his head, he could not discern between the struggling bodies of the Decentralist and Centralist.

The bodyguard went limp, then still. The old man knelt in perplexed horror while behind him, the parachutist was silent.

Suddenly a group of fishermen clambered down from the rim of the volcano. Mr. Descent saw them stare at corpse of the parachutist, whose forehead had been crushed as if by a brutal caveman. Mr. Decent's jagged rock. Then they saw the dead bodyguard, clutching the gun with Mr. Decent beside him.

The largest fisherman wrenched the gun away, grunting excitedly. "We seen a parachute come down," he told Mr. Decent. "So, we come. We broke your rule again, Mr. Decent. But good thing our canoe landed on this island. This is a … gun!"

The old man, seeing the fisherman's greedy grin, realized this was not a thoughtful man who would be satisfied with the solitude and austerity of his own Walden Pond. The others all fought to hold the weapon next.

The old man stared at the dead ex-Mayor, then down at his own thin fingers, stained with blood. He felt his idealistic beliefs shriveling. Bending over his young bodyguard's inscrutably dead face, the old man wept, feeling his power drain away.

THE LAST SURFER

A short story written in the early 1970s.
Setting: A dystopian Earth—and beyond.

H e refused to limp.

Out of step with the other executive-trainees, he strolled through their nationalized oil storage tank farm. His new wingtip shoes chewed the surfing knobs on his insteps, but he denied the pain. His savagely tanned face stared beyond the barb wire. His blue-green eyes stared beyond the waves, black with oil.

Was the ocean dying? This uncontrolled thought increased throbbing warnings in his head, but he refused to stop thinking. He wondered whether he was living in a final tragedy or a fable gone insane.

Public relations slickness decorated the ocean with rainbow iridescence. Yet the swells were shrouded with filthy oil. He bent forward.

In his mind, he surfed on an escaping wave. In his imagination, he leaned toward the tar-clotted nose of his board to gain speed. Pursued by the break and curl of the wave …

"Each of our platforms," the official chattered, extending a hairy arm, "has at least sixty producing wells. Each well casing is at least twelve inches in diameter."

The Surfer turned and did a double-take at that little receptor box. It was dribbling a few gallons of oil into the tank from sixty producing wells. His forehead wrinkled. His head ached threateningly as a question formed in his mind. No. He wouldn't let their domination of him, their infliction of mental pain, intimidate him. He hadn't lost all pride. *No Day Too Cold* was the fluorescent motto glassed on the deck of his winter surfboard.

Thinking about surfing made the pain subside. He thought about how he'd stubbornly hunch his soul-force against the wind and was still able to paddle out through the slicks, alone. The last contest-surfers gave up three years ago. Too much oil coated their boards and wetsuits. After a wipeout, his skin gleamed dark as a sea lion's from the oil, but he disdained wetsuits. Recklessly he rode storm-boomers, hamburgering himself against barnacled rocks. He wouldn't quit. He was enough of a surfer to overlook a little discomfort.

His question returned to mind. Boldly, glaring at the storage tank, he demanded: "Where's the rest of the oil going?"

"No..." The official sagged on the ladder in agony. The Surfer's fellow Junior Executive draftees clutched their heads, plugging their ears. While The Surfer also swayed, feeling as if a pitchfork had been driven through his skull, they stared at him, afraid he'd ask another unthinkable question. It was too painful to endure criticism of the Crusades spoken aloud, criticism that would incur punishment for all.

"All oil, from any platform," moaned the official's voice, "is instantly transmitted to its tank. Always. All of it."

"Or leaked into the ocean," the Last Surfer retorted, bracing himself.

Oddly, his accusation diminished his headache, as if he'd slipped away from what was important and forbidden. He blinked, confused. Perhaps it was because he had not assigned blame.

"No significant leakage." The official forced a toothy smile. "All over the world, hundreds of thousands of wells are being drilled by dozens of countries. Yet there's only a thin slick on the oceans. Relatively little oil is wasted on the water, only a few million gallons from faulty geological formations or blowouts due to human errors. None is lost from our technologically perfect liquid transmission system. All right men, back to the helibus."

The Surfer stood squinting at a yellow trickle from that little box. He thought he could produce as much after a few beers. But pipeless transmission had been deemed the ultimate step in man's creative evolution. He imagined Orville and Wilbur Wright tinkering with bicycles and kites. Inventions rose from inventions. Transportation moved faster and faster ... toward what?

Dazzling laser beams had foreshadowed three-dimensional holograms, followed by holographic phasers invented near-simultaneously in several countries. Light-transmission technology dissociated molecular components without releasing "explosive" energies. Improved holographic reassembly at the far end of a beam of light led to practical transmitters and receptors.

Now oil was being transported at the speed of light. But little seemed to be arriving at the steel receptor boxes. *That* made his head ache! His face hardened in a bronzed grin.

"Where's the rest of the oil going?" he repeated, defiantly.

The official staggered. "Don't you feel pain? What are you? Some kind of sadomasochist?" His hairy fist clenched.

But The Surfer didn't bother to raise his hands in self-defense, as no one hit anyone anymore. During the five years since the mysterious Crusades began, everyone had become so restrained, so docile, he thought either they were insane, or he was.

"I ought to have your court-martialed," the official said, his hands falling to his sides. "At least be more considerate of others. If you don't stop thinking aloud and hurting people, I'll have to put you back in the draft pot. You might be reassigned to the Coal Crusade, or worse."

The Last Surfer glanced toward the ocean, the remnant of his life. He didn't intend to be sent inland to dig and grind coal pumped into so-called liquid transmitters as a slurry. "I'll keep my mouth shut."

"That's not enough," the official said. "Don't think at all, except progressively. We've got to pump more oil out of Earth, more quickly, to be good Crusaders. The Oil Crusade is important to us all because—because—didn't I ask you to go back to the helibus?"

The Surfer followed the wandering official up the helicopter's jaw-ramp.

Back in air-conditioned offices, where he was undergoing basic training. While clipping and pasting statistics, he made the mistake of reading some of them.

Aware of contradictions, his head ached in warning. But he still muttered, "What the ... *this* report says our platforms produce six million barrels a day. But *that* report says our tank farm processes one million barrels a day. I mean—where are the other five million going?"

"Paste them on a different page," said his supervisor.

"Won't readers notice," he laughed, "a discrepancy of five million barrels of oil a day?"

"Forget it. How else can we fulfill production quotas for the Oil Crusade except by working, not thinking? I was ordered to take care of trouble-makers, but I didn't think *you'd* be such a headache."

"But I can't understand why everyone's changed so much since—"

"The Crusades saved us," she interrupted, as if afraid he would say something more painful. "Much better behaved, the world is, as if all our evil has gone away, retired. That's why all six crusades are wonderful. People all over the world are working hard and cooperating well; it's as if our personal devils have left us, gone."

"Not mine." He snorted.

"Yours, everyone's," she blurted, clutching her head. "I've been trying to help you in the Oil Crusade, but how self-sacrificing can I get?" She stomped off, muttering, "I wish I still worked in the Blood Bank Crusade."

At five o'clock, an official handed him an impressive parchment embossed with silver trucks on a field of gold derricks. "I'm sorry to issue this dishonorable discharge from the Oil Crusade. But even my secretary agrees you're not of executive caliber after all."

The Surfer's jaw dropped, surprised at her betrayal.

He read the bottom line: REPORT TO THE SULFER CRUSADE WITHIN 24 HOURS.

"I protest!" He rushed out to the parking lot. He'd heard nothing nice about the Sulfur Crusade. Crystallize sulfur was melted, becoming a stinking liquid pumped into pipeless transmitters, then sent... where?

In his disturbed condition, he drove instinctively toward the sea as if he could find escape. Although it increased his headache, he considered becoming a Crusade Invader. He winced.

On both sides of the crowded freeway lane ahead of his Volkswagen, masked intakes of the Clean Air Crusade inhaled exhaust fumes from automobiles so downtown Los Angeles air looked nearly clear as glass. He'd given up wondering where all the smog was going.

He wondered what foreign country he could escape to. But all were working like mad in the Crusades. He could be redrafted anywhere. He swerved his battered bug down the off-ramp toward Wilshire Boulevard.

Through the crisp air he could see across Santa Monica to the surf. "I won't leave." He stopped at a sporting goods store advertising a distress sale of mountain climbing equipment. "I won't leave the ocean."

As he strolled into the store, the city air seemed brisker than yesterday. Continuously sucked away, it was replaced from the sky and higher altitudes. He felt energetic and breathless, as if Los Angeles were in the mountains. Already so much air had been transmitted somewhere else that the atmosphere was noticeably rarified. Yet he knew decreasing air pressure was forcing evacuation of some older people from higher altitude cities, such as Denver.

Inside the store were wonderful bargains on mountain climbing equipment, now that oxygen tanks were no longer available except for high officials. Rock-scaling equipment was offered at giveaway prizes.

After flipping coils of rope, slings, and pulleys onto the backseat of his Volkswagen, he drove to his apartment to retrieve his oil-blackened surfboard and trunks. Although he intended to be more relevant than a Crusader Evader, he was careful not to think ahead about what to do, lest the powers that be detect those thoughts and punish him. He would postpone that headache until instinct triggered him.

While driving past Malibu, the ski tip of his Camel surfboard fluttered above the sunroof of his bug like a displaced wing-casing. Sunset glowed across acres of oily low, low, tide sand. The sea level had declined amazingly since the Clean Oceans Crusade began.

He wrapped his Marlboros and Zippo lighter in a plastic bag and stuffed them into the wax pocket of his Jantzen Jams. For a moment he noticed the chilly ocean breeze on his skin, but he had trained himself to generate inner heat. He waded through oily foam and hopped onto his board in a kneeling position, having inflated it for maximum flotation.

With quick strokes he paddled out to beat the shore-break. His board tilted up the crest of a wave, flopped over, and slithered across swells. Private boats weren't permitted here.

Silhouetted against the cloudy sunset, the oil production platforms make him think of long-legged spiders sucking Earth's blood.

He lowered his body to a prone paddling position to reduce his radar image. He wasn't sure whether those automated production platforms were guarded by radar or lies. His head throbbed with each stroke. They were certainly guarded by headaches. He rested his chin on the coils of climbing ropes he'd taped on the deck of his board. His oiled arms drove him through increasing pain.

The platform towered above him like landing areas large enough for Jupitereon modules to blast off from. Their pumps roared.

If I can overcome the pain, he thought erratically, *I'll be free ... of what?*

He peered up their oily legs. Shrieking pumps were monitored in a remote-control building at the tank farm. He hoped white-coated attendants weren't watching for red warning lights. Supposedly these deserted platforms were guarded by infrared-detecting devices. But that might be to warn of fire, not intruders.

A dull pain clubbed his head as his board bumped the nearest tar-blackened platform leg. He roped it ingeniously with self-releasing loops so he would be able to hoist his board free, quickly.

Even the lower deck seemed inaccessibly high above him. He supposed the transmitter was on the upper deck. Hopefully, he'd recognize it. Masked intakes of the Clean Air Crusade were the only transmitters he'd seen. But a friend of his, home on silicosis leave from the Coal Crusade, claimed to have seen a transmitter. "Like the sun..." he'd whispered. Uncrushed lumps of coal bigger than men's heads were sucked into a liquid transmitter as easily as coal dust slurry. His friend halted the conversation, clutching his forehead in pain, then in a monotone changed the subject. "We've surpassed our coal transmission by 186%."

The Surfer knew why everyone supported all six Crusades. Dissenting was too painful.

His head throbbed, but he held up the pulley-weighted climbing rope over the corner of the platform's lower deck and slithered it down the other side. While rigging more ropes through pulleys, warning pains gnawed inside his skull like rats, then squealed as he hoisted himself to the rusty lower deck.

Lying on the cold steel of the platform, he hauled up his surfboard hand over hand. He then held it in front of his body like a shield while maneuvering toward the corroded ladder leading to the upper deck. He blinked in the dimness.

Among the squeaking pumps, it seemed a voice in his head shrieked metallically, "Go back." When the Crusades had begun, that sort of thing drove uncooperative congressmen insane. Somehow automatic headache controls had been connected to memory cells. But he took his own pain as a clue he was getting somewhere.

He climbed the steel rungs of the glinting ladder while pumps seemed to moan, "Go home. Go home." Tall pipes from all sixty wells converged above him into a vibrating giantess oil conduit. He ignored the voice in his mind roaring "Go back," while scrambling to the upper deck.

Under the red-streaked sky, a huge pipe sprawled past the landing-bullseye for helicopters. At the far side of the platform, it floated upward into a steel box taller than a telephone booth, then ended.

He lurched toward that transmitter, despite thickening head pain. He circled the trembling transmitter and reached up to touch it. A fleeting thought enticed him to step off the edge of the towering oil platform, but his surfboard was no substitute for wings.

He stumbled over a rusty wrench a repairman had left, then reached for it. He realized if automated devices on the platform signaled trouble, a helicopter would rush men from shore to investigate. As he looked toward the tank farm on shore, the final rays from the sun seemed to ignite those distant storage tanks. He recalled tanks with undersized reception boxes, magnetically floating above them, dribbling so little oil. He yelled, "Where's the rest of the oil going?"

Beside him, the great conduit shuddered under his hand as oil rushed upward with torrential force into the transmitter. But all he saw above was a vertical beam of light—more noticeable now the sky was darkening. It was like a motionless searchlight with parallel rays. Clouds above didn't seem to obstruct transmission.

As the Earth moved, so would the transmitter's aim between the stars. Perhaps the transmitter permanently pointed at satellites hovering above Earth, acting as repeater stations to aim the oil somewhere. He began reaching for the beam, feeling heated air. Reflexively he drew back. Laser beams could burn through steel. But why weren't the side-plates of the transmitter hot?

With the wrench he tightened a bolt. He must be accomplishing something, as his headache pain became excruciating.

He blacked out.

The Surfer awoke to find himself near the edge of the platform, clinging to a small pipe. It would have been a long fall into the oily sea. He had almost dropped off.

Instead of looking back directly at the transmitter, he stared at a smaller pipe terminating in a little steel box, as small as the receptor at the tank farm. Perhaps he could use that in a diversionary action. Crawling beside the little pipe, a thin limb from the trunk of the main oil conduit, his headache returned as he reached the small transmitter and he sensed he was being warned away. He touched its steel and saw a light-hole was at its end plate, aimed horizontally toward the dark shore. At the tank farm?

On its top plate were bolt heads to which he applied his wrench. It hurt, but not as much as when he'd tried to open the big transmitter. When he pointed his wrench toward the big transmitter, the pain worsened.

His dilemma was simple. The larger pain inadvertently helped him overcome the smaller. He twisted out another bolt. Because pain was relative, he could handle more. If he had attacked the smaller transmitter first, he probably couldn't have endured it. But now he'd experienced extreme pain, so he quickly lifted the steel top-plate from the smaller transmitter. The yellowish glare inside made him squint.

A horizontal jet of oil no thicker than his finger squirted from the pipe at one end of the box. It then seemed to vanish through a fog of oil droplets into a dazzling tube of light attached to the other end-plate. He thought he could see the transmitter's cryonic gate, which neutralized excess heat from holographic phaser tubes. That extreme temperature differential was the first step in breaking apart complex oil molecules. He wondered how that process avoided nuclear explosions, with subatomic energy bars severed then separated particles converted into photon equivalents. New technological evolutions.

He decided to light up a Marlboro instead of poking his fingers into the transmitter. As he pulled his Zippo lighter from a plastic bag, his head shrieked. Still, he snapped his lighter. As it flickered, he thrust the flame to the oil. There was a puff of heat and as his hand jerked back, he heard a roar like a blowtorch inside the open transmitter box.

On shore, a fiery gladiola grew upward in the tank farm as an oil tank receptor ignited. He felt almost free, ready to attack the bigger headache, the bigger transmitter, to fight the suspicious purpose of the Crusades.

He lunged, knowing he must hurry. They'd come after him in helicopters.

He hurled the flickering lighter backward over his shoulder, where his gaze wouldn't be caught by it. The pain in his head lessened. Grunting, he turned and sprang at the transmitter as if it were an animal, clubbing it with his wrench. It clanged. He twisted the jaws of his wrench on the bolts holding its side-plate. He pulled hard on that plate under the night sky with stars and planets glinting overhead. Other men were afraid to look up. They might see the wrong planets—even the name of one had been censored by headaches. He heard rumors the face of the sky had changed, bright areas spreading like reflecting seas.

Five years had passed since space travel was inexplicably terminated, other than to place synchronous satellites above Earth. Some said those satellites were shaped like steel boxes. But telescopes were forbidden.

One last pull and the steel side-plate clanged on the deck. Inside the giant transmitter a column of oil gushed upward, exiting from a hole in the top-plate into a blinding tube of light. Oil itself never struck the top-plate. Roaring, it simply vanished when reaching the light. He leaned through a mist of escaping oil droplets and felt suction, inrushing air. Above the box, the beam was like the other searchlights in the sky. The light was painful to look at, so he looked instead at the stars.

Amidst them was the blinking red light of a descending helicopter.

Whirling in haste, he tried again to find his cigarette lighter, to light up that big transmitter, but as pain dug cloven-hooves inside his skull, his hand curled the flickering lighter inward to his naked chest. He screamed as his bare flesh burned.

In a spastic struggle with himself, he knocked the lighter away. He fell sobbing, now unable to command fire. He lay on the platform while the helicopter descended.

Its cyclonic wind whipped around the deck, hurling his forgotten surfboard like a leaf. His board struck him. He grabbed it, clung to it, shielding himself from the blinding searchlight.

The Crusader Guards' helicopter docked on deck. Silhouettes emerged at the edge of a searchlight beam, helmeted but not armed, not even with nightsticks.

Behind The Surfer, the immense transmitter continued to roar with the triumphant voice of the Crusades. His mind had betrayed him. His body squirmed helplessly. He'd failed to break free.

"Be a good boy," the guard said confidently as he approached with an empty straitjacket. Now that evil had retired from the earth, they didn't carry guns. "Be a good boy."

The Last Surfer shrank behind his board, knowing he should obediently extend his arms. But he'd have to let go of his board. He imagined himself comfortably wrapped in the straitjacket, with no more decisions to make. No more headaches if he surrendered limply. Meanwhile, the world's oil and coal and sulfur and water and blood and air were programmed away, leaving...

"Be a good boy," the guard's warm voice murmured.

The Surfer lurched away. It would be a useless dive to the water. They would merely pluck him out, then gently inter him in an asylum with other troublemakers who couldn't adjust to the Crusades. There was no place for dissent on this Earth.

He raised his surfboard like a shield. They snatched at it, and he retreated, cursing.

He suddenly remembered an old public relations story, designed to keep men out of the transmitters, emphasizing liquid transmissions. They were emphatically told: Men are builders, not passengers. But wait. For what higher purpose were these transmitters disposing of the world's resources?

Not for passengers? Why had they bothered to argue that point? He suddenly understood.

Dodging reaching arms, he plunged into the open side of the transmitter with his surfboard, slicing upward through the oil. Violently sucked up as if into a giant wave, he clung to both his board and his consciousness.

After a few minutes of disassociation, he rose up through oil and emerged from winding light.

He lay in warm oil, clinging to his board on an oil-dark sea under a gray-clotted sky. The hazy sun seemed small and weak; the air was surprisingly warm, yet smoky. He suddenly remembered he'd been reborn from an immense steel box below the surface.

Squirming onto his surfboard, he noticed it had less weight and buoyancy. This amazingly deep oil must be on top of the sea, a thick layer, offering less flotation than water. His board was so deeply awash he had to paddle from a prone position. Swells radiating from the submerged receptor box shoved his board in the direction of a smoggy coastline.

On shore, thousands of little plumes of smoke leaned into the wind. They rose from smoldering mountains on slopes above an oil-stained shoreline. The wind carried a sulfurous stink. His eyes blurred and he had a coughing fit. The stench made him wrinkle his nose.

He paddled against the hot, humid wind. It was strangely humid because the jagged land looked bone dry. The nearest promontory was naked rock. Behind it, curved ridges appeared razor sharp, as if never eroded by rain. They seemed to be rims of interlocking craters. Volcanic? They were fringed with indistinct splatter-patterns of shattered rock, perhaps blasted out by ancient meteoric bombardment. The terrain appeared nearly as inhospitable as the moon's.

In the distance, something moved. Between those fierce ridges he saw smooth hollows of reddish sand. Around small fire-mounds, the sand was stained ash-gray. Above one coal-black, glittering new mound, not yet smoking, something in the air glinted like steel. A receptor box?

The nearer he paddled to the smoggy shore, the warmer the oil seemed on his arms. With each stroke, his skin chafed against his board. Pain flared across his burned chest. He remembered holding the lighter flame against his flesh against his own will.

He suddenly realized this whole sea of oil could be ignited. He felt panicky, terrified by the thought of flames. He hoped those frightening coal-fires were safely inland from this sea of warm oil.

As a swell lifted him, he realized the size of these waves of oil. They were higher than Rincon Point on Big Wednesday. Swells of surf wrapped around a promontory and angled across the shallow bay, extending shimmering wave-walls all the way to a distant pier.

Pier? At this distance he couldn't see details through the smog. It seemed oddly low unless the sea of oil had risen recently. As he paddled toward the promontory, with each stroke the oil seemed warmer. Hot?

When the next swell elevated his board, he saw long metal pipes lying on the beach, running from smoldering piles of coal sledge to the shallows. It looked like a circulating heated-oil system to warm the sea.

A large swell lifted him closer. The shallows were bubbling. Boiling?

On the beach moved arthritic shapes, thousands of them, pointing at him. But intervening lines of hot and boiling surf seemed to bar him from the shore.

Those withered figures waved and loped along the beach in slow-motion, as if this planet's gravity was less oppressive than Earth's. Their wrinkled bodies seemed nakedly sexless. One pair clung together as if attached at the hips like Siamese twins.

From smoky mounds behind the beach, thousands more came... millions of them. Bodies crowded around coal fires as far as his eyes could see. They seemed to be trying to keep warm in this humid 90 degree heat, as if not hot enough already. And as if not humid enough, steel boxes sprayed water mist into the air. The heated atmosphere absorbed it all. Perhaps the water receptors hadn't been operating as long as air receptors. This planet had not yet experienced rain!

A big swell humped under his board. He looked back, hoping to pivot and paddle out to sea. But an even bigger wave, heading an immense set of swells, rose against the gray horizon.

He'd be caught inside. He realized he couldn't paddle out to those mountainous swells in time. The nearest was already cresting. Before his board could ascend it, the next big wave would break, rolling him into boiling shallows.

He glanced toward shore while a smaller swell humped under his board, then paddled frantically, trying to catch the wave's momentum. His board tilted down the wave's smooth shoulder, gaining speed as it steepened. Instinctively he stood up. With habitual grace he leaned into a right-slide across its gleaming face, along the flowing wall of the wave and into the bay.

The oily face of the swell was both above and below him. It stood so tall and thin, so delicately fluttering in the air, he wondered if the downward pull of gravity were only one-third of Earth's. This seemingly featherweight wave, small in comparison with the set churning in from outside, was at least a twenty-footer, beautifully hollowing its face above him.

He could do nothing but stretch his ride as long as possible across the smoothly flowing wall of oil, because along the bay the waiting shores were boiling.

He knew his Greenough Stage X fin would finally scrape bottom, and his momentum would hurl him forward into boiling oil. Even standing out here on his board he felt the wave's increasing heat. His swift planing board supported his weight above the hot oil for the moment, but eventually he'd be in the tumultuous shore-break, if he lasted that long.

He glanced behind at the roaring curl of the big wave, darkly breaking, pursuing him across the bay.

The unbroken slope of the wave teetered ahead of him. He leaned forward like a skier. His board slid down, gaining speed. The crest seem to hang above him, but didn't collapse, as if he'd found a forgiving wave. Not only did gentler gravity slow its fall, the oil had greater viscosity or cohesiveness than water. It held the sectioning face of the wave together long enough for him to make a bottom turn. With marginal momentum the surfboard carried him onward and up across the smooth face of the wave, while behind him the thundering curl broke, failing to catch him yet.

In his lengthening right-slide, he rose high. Under the lip of the wave, carving its unbroken face with the rail of his board in a swift skier's stance, he subtly underplayed his moves. He knew he looked good. Great!

Instinctively he glanced at the beach. Those rheumatic figures were tottering toward the boiling shallows, waving with feeble excitement. He felt disturbed by their geriatric haste, as he'd always feared getting old.

It wasn't pretty. Some wrinkled shapes were pairs sharing three legs. Apparently, the species had multiplied by budding rather than birth. Some failed to separate even in old age. All appeared as restless as naked pensioners. Craters bristled with thousands of them, a big audience. He made a swift cutback toward the curl, then away again in a spectacular S-curve to regain his position on the wave. There might be millions watching. There could be billions on this planet, like the people on Earth.

They clustered along the edge of the heated sea. Yet apparently the bubbling shallows were too hot, even for them. They didn't wade into that boiling oil.

On his board he had nowhere else to go. He wished he could cut out to sea, over the crest of this wave, before it folded into the plunging shore-break. But he heard bigger waves booming in. He was trapped. All he could do was stretch his last ride as long as possible.

Ahead of him, where a wave threatened to collapse like the shore-break, he saw more of the odd creatures hurrying onto the low pier. It would bar his way. Their restless herding reminded him of crowds of retired people lounging on Earth's piers even after offshore drilling had fouled the waves. On this pier, they pointed excitedly at him. He might be the only bright spot to relieve their boredom. Like tourists on Huntington Beach pier, they seemed to hope he'd fall, or worse. Would they clap if he collided with a steel piling?

The long shoulder of his wave extended ahead under the low pier. The oil hulked so high he knew there couldn't be enough clearance for him to shoot under the pier unless he rode deep in the trough. It seemed the sea's oil level had increased since the pier was constructed. If his timing was wrong, the horizontal walkway might knock his head off.

The wave swept up close to their peculiar feet. Their withered faces contorted. As if in anticipation, they shrieked.

His muscles hardened as his surfboard rushed at them. Defiantly he yelled at them and violently cut back, away. His final ride wasn't finished. He attempted a 180 degree turn away from the pier, back down the steepening face of the wave in a bottom turn toward its approaching curl. His board surged at the booming base of the falls. He would cut back again, bank farther downward off the foaming break, and fall to his right again in a wider bottom turn. If the wave broke above him, he could shoot his board between the pilings.

Instead, he did the opposite. He veered left, up into the open throat of the wave, framed by the curl. He leveled his board upward in a flamboyant last maneuver. Inside the breaking wave, the revolving tunnel appeared longer, darker, and more beautifully gleaming than any he had glimpsed on Earth. It was like his life's vortex as he banked his flexible board up within the liquid tube.

With heel pressure he activated the fin-release mechanism set in his board's deck, so the X fin pivoted, allowing his turn. He rode up the arched interior face of the tube, centrifugal force holding his feet against the bending deck during the inside loop. With a slice, he came down out of the tunnel, completing a 360 degree maneuver which would have won any best wave surfing contest on Earth.

He emerged from the interior heat and darkness, slashing out as the curl roared after him, then under the gray sky he stalled his board high on the wave. Meeting the pier, he crouched, then reached up with both hands to grab it, his body swinging underneath as his board shot between the pilings. He hoisted himself onto the pier, agonizingly aware that his legs had been splashed by hot oil and his feet were so blistered he couldn't feel whether the steel pier was hot or cold.

He recognized the trademark on the pier's girders, prefab steel that had been transmitted from Earth. He supposed some of these crowding shapes had arrived the same way before multiplying.

Their faces were ruddy with excitement as they massed around him. He wished they didn't look quite so human—that's what made seeing them so disturbing. Arthritic fingers touched him, stroked him, tried to soothe him as they jabbered in a dozen languages. Several times he recognized the words "Do it again."

Their breath was foul as if it rose from their intestines filled with blood from the Blood Bank Crusade. As they clustered around him, he suspected their favorite temperature was 98.6 degrees. He shrank from the embrace of an incompletely divided pair, three arms, two wrinkled young-old faces.

Something had gone wrong with their reproduction. If these grinning parasites of mankind had multiplied by budding rather than birth, their original DNA pattern must have deteriorated. Their species aged because there was no exchange of genes, no mating. A hell of a mess. Each generation budded older, more weathered, and weaker than the last.

For some reason, they'd left their ancestral Earth. He remembered the last manned flight to Mars had carried a fission-electric power source, a circular electromagnet, steel plates and bolts. It also contained equipment: perhaps to assemble the first hopeless "liquid" receptor here. It was supposed to facilitate men's development of this meteor-pocked planet. But headaches had begun on Earth and space flight forgotten by men.

Mankind's energies were redirected into the Crusades, with insane construction of thousands of big transmitters and few receptors on Earth. Parts for big receptors had all been transmitted here. He looked around wildly. This place was draining Earth's oil, water, air, coal, sulfur, and blood— even prefab steel peers for geriatric promenading.

Yet for those human hosts far away on Earth, as mind control by headaches operated successfully, indoctrinated men continued working blindly. They obediently did their jobs, expending their lives in the Crusades. And he?

Now withered hands clutched at him and pointed toward the surf. "Do it again," gleeful voices commanded.

Along the beach, others hobbled to retrieve his surfboard.

They clung to him, jabbering with anticipation. He backed away from their foul breaths until he was cornered against a metal-screened brazier on the pier. He recoiled. The coals inside were so hot. Excited oldsters huddled around it, yet he felt delirious in the heat. It seemed like a fiery mouth of Baal, with ancient jaws gaping for Canaanite sacrifices.

One old devil earnestly shook his hand. "We want to thank you," his decrepit voice creaked. "Thank you all, for our Retirement Heaven."

But his red face screwed up in geriatric dissatisfaction. "We need more coal."

Their petulant voices combined. "It's still too cold here." "Not nice, like in the plans." "The oil baths are too hot." "My rheumatism is worse." "The sulfur sauna hasn't cured my eczema."

"We need better entertainment," another complained with devilish discontent, "than you."

Frantically The Surfer shoved them aside. He saw how Earth would end, resources and lives frittered away.

"Ingrates, it was my greatest ride." He laughed because he understood now what he could do.

Most of his life he hadn't been afraid of dying while surfing because he thought it would be the way a surfer ought to. A loose board leaping like a salmon. A stunning blow. Clasped within his last wave was the way a surfer should die. Not by burning.

Yet he lunged at the glowing brazier, yanked off its protective screen, and punched both hands into the blistering coals. He raised them, blazing, clutching the fire as their voices screeched in warning, then dove into the surf.

His breaking wave flared up, curling flames rolling toward shore. A shimmering tube of fire burst with a blow torch roar. Beyond blinding heat, he knew he'd succeeded as the sea incinerated everything on the pier. Its fiery swell swept in on shrouding smoke around their world. Gases from burning oil mixed with the oxygen in the air. Heat rising, the increasingly explosive atmosphere ignited, a sheet of flame encompassing the planet. Clouds of smog and water vapor vanished in that fiery instant.

Mars continued in its age-old orbit but blackened. On Earth, clogged transmitters gurgled, strangled, squirted oil between steel plates. Pumps choked on the increasing pressure of oil backing up in their pipes.

Men blinked at red-flashing control panels and at each other. Without headaches, they suddenly stared at their oceans, darkening with oil, finally seeing them. What had happened to their desecrated world? For the first time, in their lifetime, they were free.

On blackened Mars, steel receptor boxes sat warped by that last tremendous flash of heat.

On desecrated Earth, platforms were dismantled, sea-sweeping began, and wide-eyed men planted trees where strip-mining had gouged out coal. They reforested mountainsides scarred by centuries of civilization. They wondered how to restore the drained atmosphere without further disturbing life's delicate balance.

When their ocean finally began to cleanse itself and waves rose blue-green, young boys paddled out uncertainly on their grandfathers' boards, unaware that anyone had died for them. Rising erect, they slid across sparkling waves, shouting with joyous discovery, thanks to The Last Surfer.

END NOTE

By
Laurie Winslow Sargent

R eaders of this volume who previously read VOL ONE
will recall that I knew Hayden Howard affectionately
as "Jack." Born and raised in Santa Barbara, California, he
was a confirmed bachelor (or so he thought) until age sixty-
four. He met my 54-year-old mother, three years after her
husband, my father, died in a tragic motorcycle accident.
Although I was already a young adult and a mother, Jack in
essence became stepfather and friend to me for twenty-five
years until his passing. At that time, he asked that I be the
executor of his estate.

This included going through his old papers, including
half-century-old hidden stories. Those manuscripts had
been buried under massive paper piles, behind a door that
could barely be nudged open. Although he passed away in
2014, it wasn't until a few years ago that I realized what
a treasure those boxes held, so set out to have his stories
republished.

Although he was actively writing travelogues and poetry
in his later years, only recently did I realize he had been
internationally known as Hayden Howard for his science
fiction in the 1960s.

He was known particularly for his 1967 Nebula
Award-nominated novel, *The Eskimo Invasion* (New York:
Ballantine Books) about a bizarre, extremely fast-breeding

population Canadian Arctic villagers—who could not have been human. In VOL ONE of Reawakened Worlds, "Arctic Invasion" is the novelette (also an award finalist) that began that novel but is a fascinating story in its own right.

Previously in magazines were several stories you read in this second volume of *Reawakened Worlds*. "Oil-Mad Bug-Eyed Monsters," was also previously in *BEST SF: 1970,* edited by Harry Harrison and Brian W. Aldiss (G.P. Putnam's Sons New York, 1971.) "To Grab Power," was reprinted in the paperback *Isaac Asimov's Wonderful Worlds of Science Fiction: 7 Space Shuttles* (edited by Isaac Asimov, Martin H. Greenberg, and Charles G. Waugh, published by New American Library, NAL Penguin Inc, 1987.) "Kendy" was originally "Kendy's World," in *Galaxy Science Fiction*, Feb. 1969, as previously mentioned, plus the French version. These three longer stories were each condensed slightly to fit in *Reawakened Worlds* Vol 2.

For those of you who have not yet read Reawakened Worlds, Vol 1:

I n Part One: WHAT IF: the first story, "The Tragedy of Henry Diddoh" (written in 1951) is set in a university town in a secret laboratory. A Frankenstein-esque experiment enables a professor to be in two places at the same time, but disastrous consequences ensue. So far this has been the reader-favorite in that volume.

The second story in Vol. One is "Ten Rounds for the All-Time Champ" (also written in 1951) in which a prize-fighter in the 1940s goes ten rounds against a stranger with an even stranger audience, in hopes of remaining the champ. Hint: time-travel is involved so watch for clues. You might also like to look up these boxers to see what years they fought in: Joe Louis, Jack Dempsey, and Jack Johnson. That will add an "ahah!" moment for you near the end of the story.

The third story is "We Specialists." The plot is eerily reminiscent of a true news story that occurred not long before the story was written in 1967. It's still familiar to many who have taken college psych courses even fifty years later. Hayden Howard reset the story in a dystopian future and makes no mention of the true story, but it is apparent.

Also in Vol. One, in Part Two: STRANGE ENCOUNTERS ON EARTH, the fourth story is "Gremmie's Reef" (written in 1964) about a young teen surfing off the coast of Santa Barbara, California who makes an unusual discovery. Fifth is "The Butcher" (written in 1951) about students working an archaeological dig in New Mexico who find something unearthly. The sixth story is the previously mentioned "Arctic Invasion" from 1966.

In Vol. One Part Three: INTERPLANETARY TALES, the seventh story is "Haranu" (written in 1950) where on Mars, an Earthman settler's innocent dog nearly gets his master killed. The man finds a more peaceful solution with the help of a Martian—but the dog now must choose between two masters. The final and eighth story in Vol. One is "Mutiny in the Orbit of Uranus" (written in the mid-1950s to '60s) where a spaceship crew attempts a takeover, culminating in a massive anti-gravity battle.

Vol. One is available in eBook, audiobook, paperback, and collectible hardcover.

For More News About John Hayden Howard, Signup For Our Newsletter:

http://wbp.bz/newsletter

Word-of-mouth is critical to an author's long-term success. If you appreciated this book please leave a review on the Amazon sales page:

https://wbp.bz/RW2

From John Hayden Howard and WildBlue Press

REAWAKENED WORLDS

In two volumes, the imaginative and thought-provoking work of the late John Hayden Howard (1925-2014), a master storyteller in the realms of dystopian and science fiction comes alive! Compiled by Laurie Winslow Sargent, these collections present Howard's tales, originally penned between the 1950s and 1970s, a period rich in science fiction innovation.

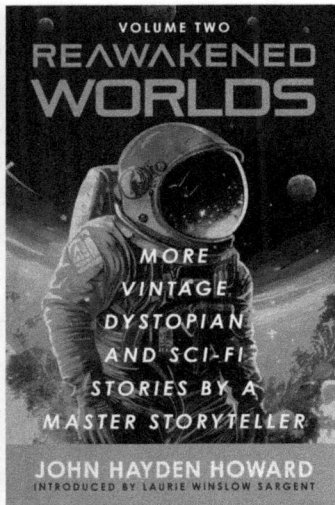

https://wbp.bz/RWwbp
https://wbp.bz/RW2wbp

More Science Fiction from WildBlue Press

The Spy-fi 'Timberwolf' Series by Tom Julian

Once a top black ops agent, Timberwolf Velez's world shatters when he encounters Kizik, a malevolent psychic alien spider that leaves a lasting mark on his psyche. Haunted by his past, Timberwolf now faces an ominous threat as a religious fanatic unearths a hidden cache of unimaginably destructive weapons. Will Timberwolf rise above his shattered mind and prevent the galaxy from descending into irreversible chaos?

With an ensemble of captivating characters and exhilarating twists at every turn, TIMBERWOLF: Book One in the Spy-Fi 'Timberwolf' Series will keep you on the edge of your seat. Brace yourself for a heart-pounding, action-packed page-turner that refuses to release its grip.

https://wbp.bz/timberwolf
https://wbp.bz/rubicon

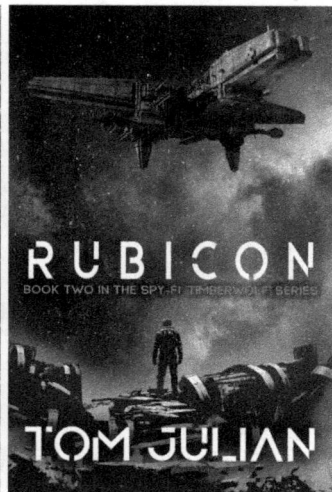

THE HAPPENSTANCE Series by Phil Sheehan

Join protagonist Blake Thompson and his friends as they navigate a world filled with alien technology, global conflicts, and unexpected dangers. From lost loved ones to treacherous encounters, they must rely on their skills and teamwork to survive. The HAPPENSTANCE series is a must-read if you love believable futuristic science fiction blended with heart-pounding action. Phil Sheehan's HAPPENSTANCE series is a captivating sci-fi saga packed with non-stop action, suspense, and multiple concurrent plots on Earth and beyond; this series demands your attention and tugs at your emotions.

http://wbp.bz/happenstancea
http://wbp.bz/tribulations

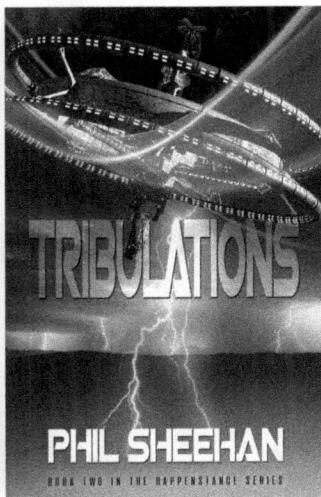

Printed in the USA
CPSIA information can be obtained
at www.ICGtesting.com
CBHW071544140824
13146CB00004B/61

9 781960 332349